Mystery ROAD

Sage —

It was an honor
and priviledge teaching
you! Good luck! Enjoy
Mystery!

ROAD

KEVIN LUCIA

CEMETERY DANCE PUBLICATIONS

Baltimore

❖ 2022 ❖

ISBN: 978-1-58767-829-5

Manufactured in the United States of America.

Cemetery Dance Publications
132-B Industry Lane
Unit 7
Forest Hill, MD 21050
Email: info@cemeterydance.con

www.cemeterydance.com

Praise for *Mystery Road*:

"*Mystery Road* is a talented author's personal variation on genre traditions. It's so clearly and elegantly written that I couldn't help but read the whole thing in one sitting."

– Mike Thorn, author of
Peel Back and See.

"*Mystery Road* is a beautifully written, poignant story about a man caring for his dying father and the memories that suddenly return to him after decades of forgetfulness."

– Char's Horror Corner

"What you have (in *Mystery Road*) is a story told very well, with raw emotion that makes it all the more powerful."

– Mark Allen Gunnells, author of
Before He Wakes

I dwell in a lonely house I know
That vanished many a summer ago
And left no trace but the cellar walls,
And a cellar in which daylight falls
And the purple-stemmed wild raspberries grow.

I dwell with a strangely aching heart
In that vanished abode there far apart
On that disused and forgotten road
That has no dust-bath now for the toad.

"Ghost House" by Robert Frost

For T. M. Wright:

Thank you for showing us our ghosts and how to face them.

1.

AFTER TWENTY YEARS of willful amnesia I finally remembered Anne Marie La Pierre several hours before Dad passed away quietly at the Webb County Assisted Living Home. He'd been ill for many months, and maybe we could've extended his life a little longer if we'd taken him to Utica General. But he'd refused up until the end, which in hindsight I suppose was better. Mom had died ten years before, Dad had lived a full life since, and even though we could've fought his Alzheimer's with any number of experimental therapies, I think he was just tired and lonely for Mom and ready to move on. At the very least, he left this Earth quietly, in relative peace.

Of course at the time, driving down Bassler Road on my way back into town to resume my bedside vigil (which, unbeknownst to me, was ending), I felt more annoyed at Dad's stubbornness than anything else.

Because it was so typical of him.

He'd decided to go and that was it and it didn't matter what we thought or how we felt about it. To me, he was indulging in a burst of deathbed selfishness, and of course in my emotional blindness, I was completely missing my own selfishness...

He was my Dad.

I didn't want him to go.

My turbulent thoughts ground to a screeching halt before the railroad tracks, however, when my car's radio hissed and crackled, The Verve's "Bittersweet Symphony" fading and flickering as another song whispered its lyrics through the static...

and I'm a million different people, from one day to the
HISSSSSS
down in the hollow
playin a new game

Instinctively I slammed on the brakes, pulling my Ford Taurus to a skidding halt along Bassler Road's gravel shoulder. I sat there for several seconds, staring at the hissing, crackling radio, and then with a slightly trembling hand, I reached out and turned the volume up, and through the static I barely heard...

HISSSSSS
you...my brown-eyed girl
yeah you....eyed girl

I shut the radio off.

Breathing heavily, my heart suddenly racing, I closed my eyes and cupped my face, rubbing my temples with my fingertips. I took another deep breath.

And I dropped my hands, opened my eyes and looked out the passenger side window, already knowing what I'd see.

A kitschy, touristy log-cabin mailbox.

Standing at the mouth of a narrow asphalt road branching off Bassler Road and running parallel to the tracks for half a mile before curving away into the woods. A road I hadn't seen on the way to town because weeds had clogged its entrance, and because the mailbox hadn't been there, either.

But now it was.

I sat there, staring.

And that was when I remembered—or allowed myself to remember—Anne Marie La Pierre.

I remembered the summer of 1990.

I remembered when I learned how unexplainable the world was, how narrow my perception of it, and how small I was in the face of it all.

1.

EVENTUALLY, WE ALL encounter the truth of how little we understand the world around us. At different times in our lives, and in different ways. For some, this truth comes during life-altering events: devastating sickness. Accidents and near death experiences. Personal or professional loss. A mid-life crisis, affairs, death of loved ones or children taken from us too soon.

For others, this truth comes through much kinder circumstances: during childbirth, marriage, or the gentle passing of a family's elder statesmen or matriarch. And for still others it comes humbly: along the rays of a red-orange sunrise burning away the morning fog, when fishing from a boat floating aimlessly in the middle of a quietly rippling lake, or hunting in the winter woods and meeting a proud twelve-point buck but staying your hand, content to share the soft, white silence with such a dignified creature.

Holding hands for the first time.

That first kiss.

All moments hinting to us that there's more to our existence than what we see.

That summer of 1990, I learned how strange and unexplainable the world really was. I was fifteen, going into tenth grade, obsessed with basketball, books and comic books, and by then secretly tinkering with a strange new thing called *writing*.

But I was just fifteen.

Had never been kissed, hadn't ever driven a car, and had never experienced death in any real or personal way (great-grandmothers I hardly knew didn't count, really).

I grew up in many different ways that summer. I got that first kiss. I drove (with disastrous, frightening and somehow still hilarious results) and I experienced death personally not only once, but unfortunately twice.

And along the way, I got into all the expected mischief of a fifteen-year-old country boy, including one memorable incident involving an exploding can of bug spray in a campfire. And, I saw many weird things I didn't understand that I just blew off because, well...I was a kid. With a healthy imagination and a willingness to suspend my disbelief.

But something else happened that summer, making me realize that everything I could learn in books, church or school could never tell me all there was to know.

That summer.

1990.

And it all happened quite by accident (or so I thought at the time) on a Tuesday morning the first week of July. I was riding my ten-speed down Bassler Road toward the Commons Trailer Park.

They had an asphalt basketball court nobody ever used and for the past two years I'd spent most my summer days there, shooting, dribbling and working on my game until Corey Bainbridge—one of my best friends since kindergarten—showed up. Then we played one-on-one until our legs turned to rubber and we had to walk our bikes home instead of riding them.

Don't get me wrong. I spent my childhood summers doing lots of other things, too: tramping through the woods, fishing, reading young adult novels and the musty detective pulp novels my great-grandmother had given me; camping out and going to the stock car races with Dad on Friday nights.

But after my first "official" basketball game as a gangly fourth grader in Webb County's Saturday Morning Youth Basketball Program, I got hooked on the game. Hoops became my drug of choice. Without it, I was nothing but a twitching junkie in constant need of a fix that could only be satisfied by a leather ball, an iron hoop and a backboard.

So playing at the Commons Trailer Park had become a daily summer ritual. Monday through Friday I woke up early, ate breakfast and before it got too hot outside split a few cords of firewood for the coming winter, a chore Dad always so considerately reserved for my "off-season conditioning."

After finishing I filled a plastic sports bottle with water, packed a small lunch, changed into shorts and a T-shirt and sneakers, stuffed my basketball into my backpack, hopped onto my ten-speed and headed out.

That day, however, something altered my plans. There I was, huffing my ten-speed up over the railroad tracks crossing Bassler Road…

When I squeezed the brakes, astonished.

Skidding my bike to a halt on the gravel shoulder.

Staring at a log cabin mailbox I'd never seen before, sitting at the mouth of a narrow road. A quick inspection revealed this wasn't the railway access road used for track repairs. That was the narrow gravel strip running alongside the tracks on the other side. This was an actual, for-real asphalt road just barely wide enough for one car or truck. A road that ran parallel to the tracks for half a mile, then curved away into woods I'd never explored before.

And that intrigued me.

See, my friends and I were pretty territorial, sticking to the woods behind our homes. We had those areas mapped out like the backs of our hands. We'd built a tree-fort behind Corey's house, an underground fort behind Gary McNamara's house, we camped out once a month behind Nate Slocum's house. We knew every nook and cranny of those woods, knew every bend and turn of their paths by heart. We also frequented a fishing and swimming hole just under Black Creek Bridge on the other side of town, down the road from the lumber mill. These areas were known to us, familiar.

So you can imagine, perhaps, how I felt at the abrupt discovery of this mysterious road branching off Bassler Road, a road I was sure I'd never seen before.

I sat there, straddling my bike, staring down that road, feeling conflicted. The Commons basketball court beckoned, my fingers itching to curve around the worn contours of my Spalding, and in an hour or so, Corey would meet me there. Those were days long before iPhones or 4G coverage, so I hadn't any way of letting him know something had held me up.

I knew, of course, that Corey would be cool if I did show up late, but this was *basketball.* Every minute not spent burning sneaker-rubber on the Commons' asphalt court perfecting my crossover move to the hoop or honing my jumper were minutes wasted.

And as I sat on my bike, staring down that mystery road, my fingers flexed and twitched on the handlebars, longing for the cool, leathery touch of my basketball.

But something else pulled me toward that mysterious road. An indefinable longing for something I didn't understand, then. A whispered promise that, hey...basketball would be there tomorrow, the next day, the day after that, and the season ahead. Basketball would be around for a while, yet. This, however...

And I wonder if, even back then; I was starting to change in small ways I could never have articulated, that even in the midst of my basketball mania my mind, heart and soul were secretly mapping out other, new paths.

Years later, halfway through a moderately successful small-college basketball career, I'd gradually lose interest in the daily grind of intense competition and wander away from the court to pursue other interests; chief among them, of course, writing and telling stories like this one.

But I think it all started back then, in the discovery of that strange road, which seemed at the time to represent a story with an unknown ending. For the first time in my life, I realized I could put the routine aside for a while, turn down that road, discover what awaited me at its end and maybe also discover something new, something hidden...

Or I could pursue the normal and expected. Do what I'd always done, what I'd done every day all summer, what I'd do every day for the rest of the summer, just like always.

I thought about it some more, mulling over my choices: business as usual, or something different. And I knew Corey would be cool with me being late or even missing altogether, as he was always cool with everything. Even though he was basketball crazy like me he was also a fifteen-year-old country-kid. He'd get it. He'd understand the road's attraction.

I checked my watch—a square, blue "Transformers" digital watch that detached from the band and unfolded into a small robot—and saw it read 11:30.

I looked back up at the mouth of that road.

And as I turned my bike and checked for traffic both ways, then crossed to the other side, I realized I'd probably never tell Corey about this. If I made it to the Commons at all today, I'd come up with an excuse for my lateness: chores, extra wood splitting (always plausible with my Dad), or something like that. If I didn't make it at all, I'd call him later with an equally serviceable excuse: Dad had *lots* of extra chores for me in the garden (again, very plausible), or my bike chain had slipped off…

Either way, even as I glided across Bassler Road, then bumped off it onto what was definitely a road, I instinctively understood that I'd never tell my friends about this, because it was private. It was mine, and not to be shared.

It did occur to me that my discovery might be nothing at all, or maybe something unpleasant, like the thirteen dead and skinned dogs Dad and I discovered last summer along the train tracks running behind our house. I shivered at the thought (my mind skittering around why anyone in their right mind would want to kill a dog or thirteen of them, much less skin them) but my course didn't waver. I was committed, determined to follow that road wherever it might lead.

7.

I BUMPED DOWN a short hill (the asphalt slightly cracked and heaving in a few places), and at the bottom the road leveled out, winding its way into the woods, leaving Bassler Road and the railroad tracks behind. A strange quiet descended as I wound deeper into the forest. I couldn't have traveled that far in such a short time, but Adirondack forests are thick, densely wooded, its trees crowded together. Easy to feel cut off from the civilized world with nothing but stands of fir, birch and Adirondack pine all around.

It wasn't too long, however, before I reached the road's end, and there stood an old house in the middle of a clearing. The road's asphalt dissolved into a gravel turnabout that looped around a dry, oval patch of dirt that might've been a flower garden once, and in a few peddle-turns I found myself shuddering to halt a few feet from the front porch.

I took a deep breath. The air smelled pure and clean, of fresh Adirondack pine. Also, in that quiet I felt a strange *watchfulness.* Reverent, respectful, like being in a church or cemetery. And then, in a flash, sitting on my bike, staring at that house…I knew, somehow, that I'd been inside, and that if I went inside…

I'd recognize things.

Which was impossible.

Because I'd never seen this house before.

But I somehow knew that immediately past the front door sat a small foyer for coats, hats, boots, and shoes. There'd also be a circular wrought iron firewood rack standing about chest-high.

Through the foyer, directly left would be a small living room with a couch, two recliners and a glass picture of Blue Mountain and Blue Mountain Lake hanging on the wall above the couch. Straight would take me past a steep staircase on the left and through a door that opened up into a dining room. On the far left of the dining room would be an old, cast iron wood stove. Against the wall closest to the stairs would be an antique armoire filled with assorted things: old plates and glasses, ceramic statues and knick-knacks…

A ceramic hobo clown.

Twirling a broken umbrella over his shoulder. And past the dining room would be the kitchen.

I'd been here before.

Which was impossible. I'd never set foot in this house, had no memories of it at all…but I *knew* what it looked like inside. And this revelation crept into my awareness as I straddled my ten-speed, feeling disconnected, numb and floating.

I toed my bike's kickstand down and dismounted. I slipped off my backpack, hung it from my bike's handlebars and slowly approached the house.

Even now the memory takes on the hazy, soft edges of a day-dream. The clearing felt deeply silent save the whispery scuffing of my Nikes on a blanket of rust-red pine needles and the high buzzing of katydids in background. And the nearer I got to that house, the more I felt as if everything in this clearing had been set on pause, everything frozen and waiting for someone to discover it, or waiting for someone to return.

I glanced at the front porch, debating whether or not I should try the front door or poke around outside. I opted for the latter and decided on a little reconnaissance first, so I circled to my left around the house to its "backyard." Not much grass really, just swathes of downy moss and patches of sandy Adirondack soil dotting a sea of pine needles. Near the edge of the clearing sat an old, rust-colored swing set that looked at least twenty years old.

And there was something about that swing set that puckered the skin on my forearms, despite the warm summer air. A slight breeze was blowing, nothing more than a summer draft... but those swings hung still, as if caught in a vacuum, as if the breeze touched everything except those swings. They seemed like the house...frozen, paused, *waiting* for something.

I shook the feeling off, telling myself how ridiculous that was, deep inside some part of me knowing it wasn't that ridiculous at all. But when I rounded the back of the house I saw something that jolted me, freezing my feet to the pine-needled ground.

Parked before an old, plain garage was a pickup truck. A 1968 Chevy. I recognized the make because I'd built several plastic models of that same truck.

Unlike the house, the swings and the garage, it looked recently used—only a few rust spots here and there—and had obviously seen a car wash recently. The tires were deep black, their rims shiny. I took several tentative steps toward the truck, all the while feeling the weight—yes, that's the right word for it, the *weight*—of the house looming behind me.

Watching.

Waiting.

And it was a curious sensation, because I wasn't exactly frightened, or even intimidated. More like...humbled. I felt very aware of something bigger, older, and deserving of my respect watching me very closely.

However, when I got close enough to peer into the truck's windows I saw a set of very ordinary keys hanging from the ignition. On the passenger seat I saw a fairly new ball cap. Couldn't see its face, but what I could see didn't look like a sports insignia. Instead, curving around the front I read what looked like the word 'Beach.' Probably bought on vacation in a tourist shop, somewhere.

Something about that hat bugged me, though. Like the house, I felt sure I'd seen it somewhere before, but I couldn't place when or where, so I dismissed the notion and moved on.

And it dawned upon me as I turned that none of this was very mysterious at all. A recently cleared drive, a truck sitting in front of a garage, keys in the ignition? Obviously this was a seasonal home someone had either just bought and was refurbishing, or was re-opening after a long time away. That realization replaced my reverent unease with a much more practical fear: the house belonged to someone who was probably in there right *now*, while I stalked around it like a no-good juvenile delinquent or, at the very least, a nosy kid trespassing on someone else's property.

Private property.

Time to hustle, pronto.

I walked quickly as possible around the house toward the front…and then froze in quiet panic. The side of the house I was on had a big sliding glass door opening up to a deck. Its curtains were pulled back (another indication of occupancy) and I could see inside clearly; see a table, a counter, what looked like an armoire…

And a flash of movement, moving past the sliding glass doors to the front door…

To cut me off from my bike.

To prevent me from leaving.

"Shit!"

I dropped all pretense and bolted for my ten-speed, which seemed like a thousand miles away.

But the race was over even as it started, because as I passed the house's front steps I heard the screen door screech open, slam shut and then heard a sound every country boy with a hunting Dad knew by heart.

The clack-CLACK of a .22 ratcheting.

"Hold it there, bucko."

My mother hadn't raised a fool. The sound of that .22 cocking and that calm but firm voice was more than enough to stop her pride and joy in his tracks. Shamefully enough, I have to admit I reached for the sky, throwing my hands up like a clichéd villain in a corny Sunday afternoon black and white Western. A curious mixture of deep embarrassment and cold fear gripped me, twisting my guts, pinching my bladder and holding me fast in my tracks.

And that cold fear was only lessened slightly when that voice snorted and said, "Oh, stop. No call for all that. Just drop your hands and turn round so I can see who's haunting my place like Casper."

I turned slowly, hands still ridiculously grasping the air above my head. My fear diminished, however, when I saw who was standing on the front porch. To this day, I'm not sure whom I'd been expecting to see, but it certainly hadn't been *her*.

She looked around my Dad's age, her black hair shot through with a strand or two of gray and pulled back into a ponytail. She wasn't "pretty" really. At least, not the "pretty" I associated with the soft, smooth and rounded face of my very young and blond math teacher, Ms. Collins (on whom I did not have a crush, at all). This woman's face looked more angular, defined, with a slightly sharp-edged nose and a firm mouth. Again, unlike Ms. Collins's gentle, soft, curved cheeks (again, no crush, not *me*), the skin of this woman's face was pulled tight over defined and pronounced (what I'd someday call aristocratic) cheekbones.

Her eyes glinted, dark and flinty. Not brown, not black, not gray, but something else like hard slate, or blue-black steel. I could see in a heartbeat those eyes didn't miss a thing—could catch a trick a mile away—and in that moment I had no doubts about her aim, feeling very glad that her gleaming and polished .22 was pointing at the ground.

She stood almost as tall as my Dad, with wide shoulders and maybe slightly wide hips, but she looked trim, the type of person who'd lived an active outdoor life. She probably hunted, fished and did other outdoor things: hiking, splitting and stacking wood, shoveling in the winter and whatever other work needed to be done around the house.

And yes, I hate to admit this, but I was fifteen after all. Basketball and books weren't the only things I thought about, so I did notice the two pleasantly full swells under her simple white t-shirt and I definitely reacted to her, but not in the average, horny adolescent way.

This was…different, somehow.

She didn't have of any Ms. Collins's soft curves or shining, flowing blond hair or bright blue eyes or gentle smiles. She also didn't look anything like the long-legged, short-skirted and busty cheerleaders all the older guys on the bus said were "easy" (at the time, I'd only the vaguest idea what that meant), and she looked nothing like the women in the Penthouse Jake Burns had swiped from Brook's Pharmacy last year.

It was something in her eyes.

And the way she stood there, holding that gun so casually, her shoulders squared, feet planted. She looked utterly confident, and to coin a phrase I'd heard from those same older boys on the bus, she looked like she "didn't take shit from nobody."

Something in her body, too, set bells ringing in my head. I sensed something tough there, strong, and everything about her seemed…complete.

Today, I'd use the word *symmetry*, I suppose. That woman possessed great symmetry, standing tall, lean and strong, modest breasts definitely full enough to catch my eye, but not ridiculous like those women in Jake's Penthouse. Even her forearms and shoulders attracted me. They definitely looked feminine but also strong and tight, maybe even stronger than my own.

There was something powerful in that woman, something bold, unrestrained, and *free*. As much as I love my wife now, I've never encountered a woman like that since.

She gave me a quick once-over, snorted again and smiled, flipping the gun up and resting its barrel casually against her shoulder. "Well, hell. You're not much more than a tadpole that's just lost its tail. You're tall, but kinda gangly. How old are you, anyway?"

Desperately wishing I could grumble a dismissive "nineteen," the best I could manage was a rasping, high-pitched, "Fifteen, ma'am. Last January."

"Huh. Sounds right." She waved at me with her free hand. "Go on, drop 'em. Before you sprain something. Nothing to be afraid of. Like I said, just wanted to see who was messing round my place." She pursed her lips, narrowed her eyes, looking thoughtful, her sharp gaze penetrating. "And just what're you doing round here, anyway?"

I dropped my hands, one going to the back of my neck and rubbing it as I stammered for an answer, looking away from her and back again, trying my best not to stare but having a hard time keeping my eyes off her all the same. "Uh. Well. I was biking down Bassler Road..."

She nodded at my ten-speed. "That's yours, obviously. Looks new. Never seen one like that, before."

That didn't make much sense, really, because though well maintained, my ten-speed was at least ten years old, bought second-hand at Handy's Pawn and Thrift. But being a grownup with a truck and all, I figured she wasn't up on new bikes and things like that. "Uh. Yeah. That's my bike, all right. Anyway, I was riding down Bassler Road, heading out to the Commons..."

Her eyes flashed, bright and alive. "Why are you going out there? Commons ain't full of nothin but trash. Worst kind of people live there. Not a place for a good-looking boy like yourself."

My face got all warm at that and I had to fight to keep myself from grinning like an idiot, though a part of me was a little confused. I know that years ago, the Commons had been really bad, but they'd cleaned it up a lot in the last few years, according to my Dad. "I was gonna meet a friend to play basketball..."

"Basketball? At the Commons? Where? Someone nail a hoop up to a tree out there?"

I frowned at this, feeling a little more confused...until I realized that, again, being a grown-up busy with grownup things she probably wouldn't know about the basketball court at the Commons, or even care. I'd only discovered it myself, two years ago, coming back from a fishing trip with Dad. That, and no one else ever seemed to play there besides Corey and me, so I figured it made sense, her not knowing much about it.

"Well, there's...anyway, I was riding over the tracks and all the brush had been cleared away and I guess that's why I'd never seen the road before...and I got curious, I guess. Never been down this way, so..."

I shrugged, realizing I had no good reason for trespassing on her property. I gestured limply at the road behind me. "So, yeah. Never knew that road was here and I got curious and all..."

I coughed, rubbed the back of my neck harder, wishing that, despite the summer's heat, I was wearing jeans or at least shorts with pockets so I could stick my hands somewhere and not flail them around like an idiot. "But I didn't mean any harm. Honest. I'll head right back to Bassler Road and take off, swear to God..."

And with that, I started back-pedaling towards my bike.

I figured she would stand there and stare me off her property as I beat a hasty retreat, but instead she snorted and grinned. "Hell, son. You're curious and like to poke around in the woods. That's just being a boy, is all. And you've obviously been raised with manners."

She turned and nodded toward the front door. "C'mon in and rest your feet for a bit. Get a Coke or 7UP or something, at least. Hot day out there, and a cold drink'll hit the spot, I figure."

For a minute, I couldn't believe my ears. Not only off the hook, but invited in for a soda, too? "Uh. I don't want to be any trouble, ma'am. Really."

"No trouble at all. Spent a fair amount of my misspent youth tramping all over God's creation, a regular Susie-Q Vagabond in blue jeans, so I know how thirsty a body can get. It'd be my pleasure. Though," she remarked with a puzzled grin over her shoulder, as she led me to her house, "How you managed to bike past my front drive and my log cabin mailbox all summer without seeing it is beyond me. Must not pay much attention to what's around you, son."

I shrugged—more relaxed, now—as I followed her. She was right about me not paying attention to some things. I'd always been something of a daydreamer. If it wasn't happening right in front of me or wasn't basketball, reading or writing, I tended to let it slip by without a moment's notice.

But even so, as I mounted front steps that seemed awfully dusty for a place someone was living in, I couldn't shake a light chill from my shoulders, knowing I hadn't seen the road and the log cabin mailbox before today because they hadn't been there to see.

And also?

She didn't seem to know that.

4.

I REPRESSED A sharp intake of breath when I followed her past the foyer, into her house.

I'd been right.

My eerie premonition about the house's interior—which had seemed so ridiculous and fanciful—was spot on. I felt another chill ripple across my shoulders as I glanced into the living room on my left, which had a couch, above which hung a big glass picture of Blue Mountain and Blue Mountain Lake at sunset. Two old recliners faced each other on either side of the room.

Then, I passed a steep flight of stairs to my left as I followed her into a small dining room. Against the far wall was a wood stove which a part of me *knew*, somehow, I'd stood near a winter long ago, warming myself…

"Pull up a chair," she waved at an older looking table with a yellowish-white Formica table-top, a table I knew I'd eaten at before. "You have lunch yet?" she tossed over her shoulder as she moved into the kitchen towards the oven, where faint sizzling pops whispered. "Hungry?"

It was 1990, Clifton Heights a small, innocent enough town. Back then no one would've thought twice about someone offering a kid a snack or a soda. And also, suddenly I *was* hungry. Absolutely ravenous. All I had in my backpack was a plastic bottle full of lukewarm water, an orange, and a baloney sandwich. The smell of cooking hamburgers, with onions frying on the side, made my stomach rumble.

Still, Mom had raised a boy with manners. Hungry as I suddenly was I didn't want to appear rude or overeager. "Well...I dunno. I don't wanna..."

The lady approached an older model electric oven, turned and waved, snatching up a spatula with the other hand, saying as she started flipping big, fat, *delicious*-looking ground-beef burgers, "Don' think on it. Was cooking lunch for my daughter's boyfriend—he was coming over to help me split firewood for the winter—but he's nowhere in sight. Course, Allie isn't around either, so I suspect they're off fooling around somewhere, as young kids will do."

She looked at me and smiled, warm and friendly, and nodded at the kitchen table as she worked on the burgers. "Have a seat. They're almost done."

I pulled a chair out and sat down, thinking mostly about the burgers and how it'd been a few weeks since I'd eaten a really good one, but something else kept bothering me, too. In my quick tour around the property, I hadn't seen any firewood in need of splitting, nor stacks of split wood, either. I hadn't really looked all that closely at the tree line, of course, or in the woods beyond, but still...

While I waited for her to finish the burgers she whistled a vaguely familiar tune from a popular but older song I couldn't quite remember. I glanced around the dining room, trying to ignore a creeping sensation of cold, prickly unease. There, to my left, against the wall, stood the armoire I'd somehow known would be there, stuffed with all sorts of things. Older plates that looked a bit fancy but not really valuable, teacups and glasses, knick-knacks and little ceramic salt and pepper shakers in the shapes of animals: a raccoon, a beaver and a rabbit in particular; and there on the third shelf I saw it, jammed between two stacks of dishes...

A ceramic hobo clown.

Wearing a slouch hat, twirling a broken umbrella over its shoulder, a comic-sad expression drooping on its long, sagging, narrow face.

Just like I'd imagined, outside.

I pressed my lips together and looked away, down at the cracked, slightly yellowed Formica tabletop, which I drummed lightly with my fingertips, thinking furiously.

It didn't mean anything.

That clown was the kind of cheap knick-knack every grandmother everywhere had stuffed in their overflowing armoires and even though neither of my grandmothers had ceramic clowns in their overcrowded antique armoires I figured I'd probably seen something like it at Handy's Pawn and Thrift, and...

And suddenly I wanted to leave, wanted to get out of that place, because things didn't add up. Even for a daydreamer like myself who admittedly didn't pay close attention to things, I was certainly paying attention now.

To a log cabin mailbox I knew I hadn't ever seen.

To a mysterious road that hadn't been there before today.

And a house I'd never heard of, down here by the tracks; a house that, inside and out, looked strangely abandoned but preserved...

And the lady, herself.

That woman who was somehow more attractive than my math teacher or those "easy" cheerleaders but who also seemed...*off.*

A little sad?

Lost? Lonely, even. Something about her didn't make sense, there in that house, at all.

"Here you go."

A plate appeared before me. On it sat perhaps the most delicious-looking burger I'd ever seen, freshly-cooked and still seeping some juices, sitting on a big sesame-seed bun with lettuce, a sliced tomato and grilled onions on the plate next to it.

A ketchup bottle—Heinz, my favorite, though the label looked a little strange for some reason—plunked down next to the plate. "You want that, or mustard?"

"Thanks," I said, reaching tentatively for the Heinz, not wanting to abandon my manners completely, but *very* hungry now, "I'm good."

"If you're still hungry after that one, just say so," she said, walking back to the fridge which, like everything else in the house, looked old. More rounded, almost oval. "I made a few of them, expecting young Mister Ellison and my daughter to be here. They're not, so we get the goods, I guess. Their loss, our gain."

I'd arranged the burger and fixings, tapped a blot of ketchup out, had the top bun on, the burger up and in my mouth before it struck me, what she'd said...

young Mister Ellison and my daughter

Mister Ellison

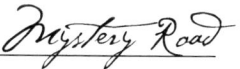

I forced myself to chew slowly, turning that name over and over in my head, another chill—more demanding, this time— flitting down the back of my neck.

Mister Ellison

Mister Ellison and my daughter

Ellison

She'd obviously added the *mister* as an affectation, because based on her middle-aged appearance, her daughter couldn't have been more than eighteen or nineteen years old, so this "Mister Ellison" had to be around the same age. But…Ellison.

That was my last name.

Ellison.

Kevin Ellison.

So who was this Mister Ellison? No one living around here had that last name other than my family. Dad's siblings had been girls, and were now married and moved away. The only other Ellisons I knew of were some distant cousins that lived downstate in Castle Creek, near Binghamton, and…

"Coke or 7UP?"

I looked up, mid-chew and mid-thought…and stared.

At two old-fashioned soda bottles she held by their necks. One of them was a Coke, which didn't look so strange, really. I'd seen a lot of those, along with Pepsi and Dr. Pepper. Some older vending machines still dispensed them. I knew this because the teacher's lounge in my school had one of those old machines and occasionally I slipped in there after hours (on pretense of looking for a teacher to ask about a homework assignment) to buy them, not just because they were only a quarter. I'd started a collection of them at home on my "stuff shelf" in my bedroom: two Pepsi's, a Coke and a Dr. Pepper.

But the other bottle she held.

An emerald green 7UP bottle. Glimmering in the light, like exotic, alien green glass. And its broad, rectangular label looked stenciled or painted on, with a big number 7 and an UP with an arrow pointing skyward next to it, and around the 7UP bubbles rose, along with these little green people swimming upward.

And it had a slogan I'd never heard before. Across the top of the label it read: "YOU LIKE IT" and along the bottom it read "IT LIKES YOU."

I swallowed my mouthful and mumbled "7UP." She handed me the bottle and I held it for a moment, savoring the touch of the frigid, smooth glass against my skin, rubbing that painted-on label with my thumb.

"You okay?"

I glanced at her, she was smiling...but also frowning, too, as if puzzled by my reaction. "Yeah," I managed, glancing back at the bottle, "I...uh, I guess I've just never seen...uh..."

I held up the bottle and shrugged. "Neat bottle." She looked at me like I was all kinds of crazy, like maybe I'd gotten too much sun on my ride down Bassler Road. I shrugged again, smiled like an idiot, and took a swig.

And my.

It tasted like sparkling, citrus heaven in my mouth, biting and deliciously cold.

As I swallowed that lovely, fizzy 7UP—which had more kick than any soda I'd ever drank—she turned to her burger and fixed it up like mine. When she finished, she reached for the slightly-weird looking Heinz bottle and asked "So, fifteen years old, huh? Makes you a...ninth grader? Sophomore?"

I took another swig of that delightful soda-that-was-nec-tar-of-the-gods, washing down another mouthful of burger. "Sophomore. Going to be, I mean."

"Huh." She picked up her burger and paused, fixing me with an inquisitive look. "Maybe you know my daughter's boyfriend, then. He's going to be a senior this year. Name's Brian. Brian Ellison. Ring a bell?"

Even now, I'm glad my mouth hadn't been full of soda or food when she asked me that. As it was I had a hard time keeping a straight face, a *very* hard time setting my 7UP bottle down on the slightly cracked, yellowed Formica tabletop without dropping or spilling it. Luckily, she bit into her burger, distracted for a moment, as frenzied confusion tumbled around in my head.

Ellison

Brian Ellison

Brian, Brian Ellison

Ring a bell?

Well, yeah. Yeah, it did.

Because Brian Ellison was my *dad*.

5.

BRIAN ELLISON.

Dad.

No.

Not possible.

Had to be another Ellison, somehow. A cousin I'd never met, or something...

maybe you know my daughter's boyfriend

he's going to be a senior this year

"So. You know him?"

The lady took another bite of her burger and chewed, watching me, waiting, looking deeply thoughtful, as if I were a puzzle she was trying to decipher. "Uh." I held the remains of my burger but didn't bite into it, not trusting myself then with another mouthful. "Think so. He play sports?"

"Sure does. Basketball, Clifton Heights varsity. Must be you don't go to the games? But didn't you say you played ball?"

I just kept staring, speechless, my mind spinning, so she shrugged, sipped from her Coke, swallowed and continued. "He was the leading scorer and MVP last year. All-Conference, too. Had a bunch of big-college offers on the table but he decided to stay local, at Webb Community. Thinks he might transfer to either Buffalo State or Harper College in two years."

I nodded, feeling numb, maybe even a bit woozy and fighting not to show it. Dad had ended up attending Webb County Community College and he'd led them in scoring his two years there, helping them win a regional championship, as well as earning them a berth in the National Tournament his second year. He'd finished a solid basketball career and his education downstate at Harper College in Binghamton.

"C'mon, you gotta know him. He's the big man on campus at Clifton Heights High."

"Yeah," I managed to say without stuttering or mumbling, "I... yeah, I do. Know him, sorta. Seen him around." And unbelievably enough, because I was somehow still hungry, I took another modest bite of my hamburger. To my relief, I found that—despite all the weirdness—I could still eat. Testimony to the resilience of a fifteen-year old's stomach in times of duress, I suppose.

I chewed, swallowed and said, "He...Brian...he come over here a lot? I mean...besides to see your daughter?"

The lady took another bite, chewed and swallowed, then said, "Sure. He comes around a lot on his own. He's a good kid. Been dating Allie about four years now, and he isn't afraid of hard work. *Mostly*, I think he's just trying to impress his girlfriend's mom," she smirked, set her Coke down and waggled a finger, "which is *not* a bad thing. Not enough young men today as worried about that as there should be. Anyway, he seems to like helping out. His Ma..."

She paused.

A troubled, slightly guilty look passed over her face, shadowing her eyes.

And then, I think, I knew.

This *was* happening. It was impossible...but it was.

I swallowed down a lump of burger and managed a slightly squeaky, "What?"

She took a bite, chewed it thoughtfully, looking conflicted. Finally she swallowed, shrugged and said, "Brian's real Ma died when he was six. She doted on him something fierce while she was alive, though; and he was real close to her. A regular Momma's Boy, and he took her death pretty hard. His Dad remarried a few years later, some city girl who'd moved here, and I suppose she's a fine woman and all...but she and Brian just don't mix. Haven't since day one. Just oil and water, I guess. She's got some ideas bout how children should be raised, about what young men should be interested in, and..."

She looked up at me, then.

And I could see it in her eyes.

A deep, lingering sadness. Not for herself, but for this young man (who was also, inexplicably, my *dad*) named Brian Ellison who didn't get along with his stepmother. "Well, he comes around here mostly for my girl Allie, and that's just fine. He's a good boy, and he's been good for my girl. But I think he likes helping out around here because he feels at home, I suppose. Like he belongs here."

She waved a hand, picked up her plate to eat the last bit of her burger, but paused and said, "I'm not gonna say I've 'adopted' him cause Lord knows I don't wanna steal him away from his home. But the sad thing is I don't think his step-momma even really cares that much. I..."

She shrugged. "He's a good boy. He's been good to Allie and if they stay together or part he'll always have a place at my table."

She ate the rest of her burger.

And I did too, my mind spinning the entire time. Because Dad's mom—Evelyn Ellis—died when he was six years old. *His* dad, my Grandpa Ellison, remarried a few years later, a schoolteacher who'd just moved to town from Syracuse, a Lucille Bevins, whom I'd come to know as Grandma Ellison. And though Dad had never, ever said a bad word about Grandma Ellison, never denied her anything she wanted or needed, so much became clearer at that moment.

Like why Dad always called Grandma Ellison 'Mother' but called Grandpa Ellison 'Pop.' Why Dad always seemed so warm and carefree—almost goofy—and on the verge of laughter around Grandpa but so quiet, reserved and almost formal around Grandma. Sitting in that kitchen, finishing probably the best hamburger I'd ever eaten, drinking mystical 7UP from a soda bottle unlike anything I'd ever seen before in that strangely familiar house, feeling at home with a woman I didn't know, I understood something which scared me a little, and also made me feel sad.

Dad had loved his father—Grandpa—with all his heart and soul. Had loved being with him, had felt free to be himself around him, and that's why I'd seen Dad cry so hard—the one and only time I've ever seen him cry—last year at Grandpa's funeral. Grandma Ellison, however—*Mother*—he "loved" because he was supposed to, because it was expected of him, because it was his duty.

And a cold, very grown-up realization struck me: that when Grandma Ellison finally passed there'd be no tears from Dad.

It was sadder than anything I'd ever heard of. Even as a

fifteen-year-old kid obsessed with basketball and books, I some-how understood.

And just like that, as I finished my burger, something inside said it was time to leave. I couldn't have put the feeling into words, really. Hell, I was only fifteen. And I'm not sure I can put it into words even now. I just understood this: that I'd been brought there for something and now that something was over and it was time to go.

And I think she knew that too, in her own way. She'd fin-ished her burger and was now sipping from her Coke, looking aimlessly out the sliding glass door as if lost in thought, like she'd forgotten I was there. She made no move to do anything with the leftover hamburgers sitting on the plate next to the stove, she just seemed frozen there. Stuck. As if she'd done or said what she was supposed to and now didn't know what to do next.

I brushed my hands off, clapping them a little.

Not a blink. She just took another sip and kept staring.

I wiped my hands on my thighs, coughed, clearing my throat, and stood.

No blink.

Just another sip of that Coke.

Finally, after, fidgeting for several minutes while she leaned against the counter, staring out the sliding glass doors, sipping her Coke, I cleared my throat louder and said, "Ma'am. I'm gonna head out, now. My dad'll be wondering where I am, and…"

That wasn't necessarily true, of course. Dad would expect me to be up at the Commons for several more hours. And yet, at that moment, I realized how timeless that kitchen and house felt. Really, I had no idea how long I'd hung around here. It felt like thirty, forty minutes, but for all I could tell, it might've been hours, or...

I noticed a clock above the counter, its hands set on 11:30.

I glanced at my blue Transformers watch.

11:30.

The time I'd read when I'd finally decided to explore the mystery road.

Forever.

It felt like I'd been sitting there forever. It was crazy, but at that moment I felt like I'd been sitting there at that cracked and yellowed table eating a hamburger and drinking a 7UP forever. And if I didn't leave, soon...

"Ma'am?"

And like something had flipped a switch inside her, the lady snapped back to life. She yawned, blinked her eyes as if rousing herself from a deep sleep, then offered me a wide, pleasant grin. "Sorry about that. Must be getting old, drifting off easier and easier these days. Anyway...yeah, you probably should get home...*Kevin*. That's your name, right?"

I smiled and nodded, trying very hard not to shiver.

Because I hadn't told her my name.

"Anyway...you need anything for the road? Apple or something?"

I started to shake my head, but then reached a tentative hand and grabbed that strange, exotic-looking emerald-green 7UP bottle by its smooth, cool neck. "Actually...can I take this?"

She waved a hand, looking surprised I'd bothered to ask. "No problem. Hot day out there, sure enough." She nodded toward the back porch, behind the kitchen. "Got some things need tending to. See yourself out okay?"

I nodded again. "Sure. Thanks for the burger. Best I've ever eaten, I think."

As I turned to leave, she said, "Oh, by the way. I can't remember. Did you say you knew Brian Ellison?"

I looked at her once more and swallowed. She appeared to be asking a simple question and didn't seem to understand just *what* she was asking. To her, it was just a question. To me?

So much more.

Because at that moment, even in the midst of all that wonderful, bizarre—and scary—weirdness, I'd learned something: apparently, I *didn't* know who Brian Ellison was. Not completely.

Maybe not at all.

Somehow I managed a weak smile. "Yeah. Seen him around. He's older than me, though."

And boy.

Was that ever the truth.

And something happened to her face, just then. It became somber, still, her eyes dark and deep like bottomless pools of water. She smiled so sadly, sadder than just about anything I'd ever seen until then, sadder than anything I've seen, since.

And when she spoke, her voice vibrated with strength, purpose and power, and also?

Love.

A mother's love.

"Well, you ever run into him, you tell him I'm not mad, okay? Even though he didn't show up. I'm not mad, an could never be mad...and that he's a good boy. He'll *always* be a good boy."

And then, I think...she knew. Or suspected, at least, what was happening here and what she was asking me to say to *him*.

Brian Ellison.

My Dad.

But I just nodded. "Sure. I'll tell him."

She smiled.

But made no move toward the back porch. She just stood there, arms crossed over her chest. So I smiled again, turned and slipped down that short hall, ignoring the steep flight of steps to the second floor, ignoring the living room and going out the front door, down the front steps, toward my bike.

And I didn't look back.

Because something told me I didn't want to see her face.

To see if she finally *understood*.

6.

I WALKED MY bike back up that asphalt road as it wound away from that house in the woods and along the tracks, steering with one hand, sipping that amazingly cool and crisp 7UP from that strangely exotic emerald-green bottle. Thoughts spun around in my head but I didn't try to sort them out or try to make any sense out of them. I just let those thoughts spin and jumble like socks in the dryer on tumble-dry, sipping my soda, enjoying the quiet woods around me and the warm sun on my skin as it poked through the tree cover as I neared Bassler Road.

And when I did pull my bike onto Bassler Road, I stopped and stared at that log cabin mailbox, its front "door" hanging open, rolled up newspaper sticking out of it.

I stared at that newspaper for several long minutes. Then I finished my magnificent 7UP with one long pull. Swallowed. Unzipped the backpack dangling from my bike's handlebars, stuffed that 7UP bottle in there for safekeeping, zipped the pack up, took it off the handle bars, slung its straps over my shoulders and set out for home. I'd meet Corey for basketball tomorrow or the next day.

Because I had something more *important* to do, right now.

7.

MY RIDE BACK home proved uneventful, lasting maybe twenty minutes. The sun warmed my back and neck, offset by a breeze. The woods on either side of Bassler Road lay quiet and still, save the high-pitched buzzing of katydids merging with the hum of my bike's tires on asphalt.

I tried not to think about what had just happened. I just pedaled, questions burning in my head, questions I needed to ask Dad, if he hadn't yet headed over to Booneville for the day.

Questions.

Questions that needed answering. Because I needed to know. And I wonder if this was the original catalyst prompting me to explore myself through writing...the need to *know*.

I turned left onto Allen Road. We lived about ten miles out of town, about five miles off Bassler Road, with about an acre and a half of property. Back then, we had just the house—a one story Concord—a garage, a small greenhouse attached to the garage and a tool shed out back. Over the years, Dad would end up adding a wood shop, two more tool buildings, a second garage for the tractor he'd buy someday, two chicken coops and a goat pen, and an honest-to-goodness barn, built from the two hundred year old beams he'd someday salvage from a barn up the road that would eventually collapse in a few years. This would all come after I graduated from college, however, before he quit teaching to open his own used book store, Arcane Delights, which I now own.

I pulled into our gravel driveway and saw that, luckily enough, Dad hadn't left yet, his black Ford pickup still parked in the drive with its trailer carrying his riding lawn mower, rakes, lawn sweeper, weed-whacker and the other assorted lawn tools he used.

Behind the trailer, I saw Dad kneeling at the trailer's tailgate, fiddling with the latch. It hadn't been working right all summer, not latching properly, so he always had to monkey with it for a few minutes before heading out to a job to make sure he didn't end up spreading his tools all over the road.

Lucky for me the latch had given him extra trouble that morning, holding him up long enough for me to catch him, because I believe that if I hadn't asked him about that house right then and there I very likely wouldn't have worked up enough courage later to do so, after I'd had time to think about it some more.

I hit the brakes and shuddered to a stop next to the trailer, kicking up a cloud of dust. Dad grunted without looking up, still fiddling with the trailer's latch. "Hey pal. Back a little early. Give me a minute here, will you? This thing's being extra stubborn today."

Still a little tongue-tied and numb from what I'd experienced, still working out *exactly* what I was going to ask him, I swallowed and mumbled something like, "Yeah, no problem." I stood there, straddling my bike, all those crazy, impossible thoughts spinning around in my head as I watched Dad work.

Dad taught high school English, but not at Clifton Heights High, where I attended. He taught at All Saints High, the small Catholic School on the other side of town. In some ways, I was glad I didn't attend All Saints, because I wasn't sure if the lines would've blurred too much at home between "Dad" and "Mr. Ellison." Sometimes, though, I thought it might have been cool, seeing a side of Dad I didn't regularly see, him talking about the literature and poetry I knew he loved.

With another grunt, Dad banged the tailgate shut, shook it a few times to make sure it held and stood, wiping his hands. He looked at me and offered his trademark, easy smile. "What's up? Everything okay? You and Corey are usually hard at it by now."

I opened my mouth...but nothing came out. The words stuck in my throat as I gaped at the battered, worn and faded ball cap Dad was wearing, a cap I'd seen him wearing to lawn jobs dozens of times over the years. All my life, really.

And it was the same cap I'd seen resting on the passenger seat of that old truck outside that house in the woods. Battered, ashen gray, the bill broken and curved until the sides almost touched, the bill's edge frayed and torn in places...but I recognized the white lettering, now. Rehoboth Beach. A hat Dad always said a "dear friend" had gotten him as a souvenir when he was in college.

Apparently, that dear friend had been the woman living in that house in the woods. And the hat in the truck had been brand new.

"That hat," I blurted, my voice amazingly even and clear. "She gave you that, didn't she? That lady in that house near the tracks, off Bassler Road. She got it for you when you were in college."

Quiet amazement spread over Dad's face, his eyes widening slightly, lips parting, as if he was about to speak but couldn't. He stared at me, amazed...no, better yet, *flabbergasted.* My dad, the epitome of calm...stunned speechless.

I was amazed at his reaction.

And quite frankly, a bit scared.

Finally, he licked his lips and said, "Yes. A going-away gift, before I left for Harper College. But how'd you...how *could* you..?"

"Dad. Who *was* she? She and her daughter, Allie?"

His jaw dropped. And I know that description is over-used, even clichéd, but that's the only way to describe it. His lower jaw dropped as he gaped at me in an astonishment that held a little fear, too, I think, and before that look totally threw me off guard, I plunged ahead, gabbing like a Chatty Cathy doll whose string had been yanked once too often. "So, I guess the road crew was out cleaning brush or something along Bassler Road cause I found this...this *road* next to the tracks I'd never seen before and it followed the tracks for awhile then went back into the woods to this old house and..."

"The house. At the end of that road. You went there?"

Dad's flashing eyes and tight face worried me because I couldn't tell whether or not he was angry. While I'd gotten into trouble before (all the usual boy-mischief) and had been punished accordingly, I hadn't ever seen Dad actually *angry* at me.

"Dad..." I swallowed, made myself meet his gaze and said, "I'm sorry. I didn't mean to. I'd just never seen that road before and I was curious…and then that house looked so weird, like no one had lived in it for years but it still looked like it was in good shape, like it was just waiting for someone to come back and I never would've gone inside if…"

"You went *inside*? How? Kevin Ellison, *tell* me you didn't break into that house, or…"

"No! She invited me in, I swear!"

"What?" He frowned, confusion seeping into his agitation. "She invited you in? *Who* invited you in? A squatter, or something? Kevin, that house is private property and…"

The phone in the garage rang.

And maybe I imagined it, maybe I'm imagining it still, my memory colored by the intervening years and my own sense of the fantastic, but that ringing sounded…different. Insistent. Dad wasn't one to let himself get distracted from something; he'd usually ignore a ringing phone in a situation like this but that ringing sounded different. Like it was ringing on purpose. For *him*.

Maybe he thought the call was the job in Booneville, canceling. Or someone calling to make an appointment for another job. Who knows? But as that phone kept ringing—and *ringing*—he held up a finger and said to me: "Wait. Wait *right here*."

He walked in quick strides over to the garage and snatched the phone off its wall jack. And even now, after all these years, I can see in my head how still he went. How the color drained from his face and how he looked at me, his face painted with a kind of fearful wonder.

"I understand," he whispered into the phone, turning to stare at me, his eyes wide and unblinking. "Thanks for calling. Yes. I'll call her, tell her the news, and will call back later today to make all the arrangements."

And with a trembling hand, which perhaps startled me more than anything else, he hung up the phone. Walked toward me, past me, head down, to the hitch at the back of his truck. He lowered the trailer's hitch-stand down and unhooked the trailer from the truck. He stood and looked at me. His face pale, eyes wide, he whispered, "Hop in."

8.

TWENTY MINUTES LATER Dad and I stood before that house at the end of the road in the woods, but it wasn't the same one I'd been in not even an hour ago. *This* house had been abandoned long ago, its windows boarded up, its exterior siding cracked, peeling and mottled dark brown in moldering stretches of rot. The front steps had crumbled into pieces, the front porch sagging in the middle.

Alongside leaned what remained of the garage. Several spots of its roof had caved in, where the snow had weighed too heavy during past winters. Its windows were likewise boarded up, as was the garage door itself.

That truck still sat in the driveway but rust had eaten away at its fenders, doors and hood. The truck's front window was cracked in several places, its grill missing—as were its hub caps—probably victims of thieving scrap-metal scavengers years ago. And the truck leaned sideways on four flat, cracked, brittle-looking blobs of old gray rubber you could only passingly call tires.

Out around the other side of the house, at the edge of the property where the swing-set *should've* been, lay nothing more than a wrecked frame of rusted pipes that had collapsed inward long ago, the bones of a dead thing.

And when Dad had stopped the truck on Bassler Road without me telling him where—like he knew the spot by heart—I'd received my first and perhaps greatest shock: weeds, brush and thick-tangled bramble clogged the entrance of that road, which we had to clear before Dad could slowly drive his truck down a much rockier, more cracked and uneven road than I remembered from an hour ago.

And there'd been no log cabin mailbox.

Dad tossed his keys into the air, caught them, then moved toward the front door. I followed. With an absent-minded "watch your step" over his shoulder, he mounted the front porch and, to my amazement, produced a key on his key-chain, inserted it into the doorknob and unlocked the front door.

I followed him inside and the odor hit me instantly: that of damp, rotten things. Stale and fungal. Before, it had merely smelled…old. Unused. Now—as our steps made slight *squishing* sounds in what remained of the carpet—it smelled *dead*.

I didn't look into the living room as I followed Dad into the kitchen. Even today, I don't know why. Maybe I just didn't want to see it changed, its sofa and chairs ragged, rotting, springs sticking out, sodden stuffing spilled everywhere.

And I'm glad I didn't look, because the kitchen proved bad enough. Almost too much, really. The wood stove and the range in the kitchen were gone. The fridge was still there, but its

door hung open, its inside bare and stained yellow by age. And scattered everywhere, all over the floor, were bits and pieces of debris: branches, leaves, acorns, twigs, all the things small animals gather to build nests and eat.

What little wallpaper remaining was peeled and stained. But the kitchen table still stood, and its old chairs sat around it, oddly looking like *someone* had just gotten up and left.

Someone like me.

Someone who had *just* eaten at this table thirty minutes ago. And on the kitchen counter, looking as if someone had finished drinking from it not ten minutes ago, sat an old fashioned Coke bottle.

Dad pulled a chair out, sat down, folded his hands on the table and nodded to the other chair. "Have a seat."

I sat down and tried my best not to look around, because all of this was bordering on sensory overload. The house before had seemed unused and mildly neglected. Now, with these stained walls, cluttered, damp and dark rooms, the air smelling foul and rotten?

Dead.

This house was dead.

"Allison La Pierre and I were best friends," Dad said without preamble, glancing at me and then looking at the sliding glass doors, which had been boarded up, also. "Long before we dated, we were best friends. Grew up together, really."

He sat back in his chair and regarded the table quietly for several minutes before continuing. "Allie's Dad died in Vietnam. Her mom—Anne Marie—never remarried, for some reason. I never knew why. But, she was a strong woman. Independent. So maybe she'd decided she'd loved one man, and when he died she decided she didn't need another to survive."

Thinking of those gray, intense eyes and steady, sure hand holding a shotgun, I didn't doubt that at all.

"I spent a lot of time here," Dad said, "in this house, playing out back, having lunch at this table with Allie and her mom." He eyed me with a small grin. "Never tell your mother this, but Anne Marie La Pierre made the best hamburgers I've ever tasted."

I returned his smile. He'd get no argument from me there.

"As time passed, I did more than just spend time here with Allie. I started helping Anne Marie with the chores. Splitting wood, staining the garage, painting the house, hoeing and planting her garden, mowing what little grass she had. And she always insisted on paying me, never tried to take advantage of my relationship with Allie."

And something grew in me, just then.

An understanding of something bigger, wider than my limited, narrow perspective of the world...almost like the first *grownup* thought I'd ever had. "But it was more than just the money...wasn't it?"

He looked at me again and smiled a little sadly, this time. "Yeah, it was. Mother and I...we never really got along well. I've always tried not to let it show, *and...*" he pointed at me, looking mildly stern, "you will never, *ever* show anything but the utmost respect and love for your Grandma Lucille, you hear?"

I nodded. He relaxed and continued. "It's just that...we weren't ever close. Maybe I just remembered too much of Mom before she died, even though I'd only been six when it happened. But it was more than that, I think. Mother—Grandma Lucille—was a city girl and she had some real particular ideas about raising children. She thought Pop—Grandpa—had been too soft and free with me, too laid back. She always stopped short of accusing Mom of the same thing...but I wonder. I wonder if she felt that way about Mom, too."

He waved that off. "Anyway. We never saw eye to eye and I couldn't seem to stay out of her way. Always in trouble for one thing or another, for being too reckless, or careless and wild, or not acting my age. Got so I was always watching my step around home, trying to stay out of trouble, mostly so I wouldn't get *Pop* in trouble."

He shook his head. "But Anne Marie? She treated me different. I never once thought I could take liberties with her but she let me be *me*. Let me breathe, even though I never dared step out of line around her. Long before Allie and I started dating, I felt...accepted here, in this house. Like I belonged. She accepted me for what I was."

"Like a son," I whispered, because with all the conflicting emotions surging inside me, I didn't dare speak any louder.

He nodded. "Yes. But she was careful not to abuse that. Didn't want Mother thinking she was encroaching where she shouldn't, trying to 'steal' her son away. I think that's why she always paid me so well for any work I did around the house. Made things more official. Made it easier for Mother to accept, too."

"But you and Allie broke up. And you still..."

"Allie and I decided after our freshmen years apart in college—me staying local and her down in Pennsylvania—that we were different people and wanted different things. I'm not going to lie; it wasn't easy. And I'm sure I probably held on to what we'd had a little too long and a little tighter than I should've, because at the time she'd been all I'd known of love, I guess. But we eventually parted as friends. And, since Allie took to staying away more and more, working summers in her college town, I kept coming around here, helping around the house, sometimes just sitting at this table eating those hamburgers, talking with Anne Marie about life and just about everything else under the sun."

Dad smiled slightly. "Again, please don't ever tell your Grandmother this, but at a time when a young man should be asking his mother questions about life, I was asking them of Anne Marie."

A strange idea occurred to me just then, one I wasn't sure I wanted to consider, because it was bizarre and weird and... well...maybe even a little...gross. Strange enough to think about Dad 'in love' with someone else besides Mom, but beyond strange to think that...maybe...maybe...

I didn't want to think about that, but also couldn't forget *her*: those flashing eyes, black hair shot through with strands of gray; her tight, firm, *fierce* face, her...essence, I suppose. Humming with an indefinable *something* that no girl I knew had. So I wondered—though I *really* didn't want to think about it—I wondered, in spite of its weirdness...

"Dad. Uh. Did you...after Allie and you broke up, and you came out here by yourself and were older and it was just you and...her. Did you ever...I mean, did you..?"

Dad's wide-eyed, slightly gaping expression of naked surprise shocked me so much I feared I'd crossed a line. But he smiled, chuckled, and pushed his cap up higher on his forehead. "Whew. You *are* growing up on me, aren't you? Fast, too. Don't know if I'd ever think to ask my Dad something like *that*, when I was your age."

His smile faded a bit, however, his eyes clouding over slightly, looking troubled. "I'm not going to lie. I think some folks did talk, said some unsavory things about the situation, but the thing was, people had always thought and said unsavory things about Anne Marie in general. In fact, I think if she hadn't paid me to do all that work—which I would've done anyway—I don't think my mother would've allowed me to come over as much as I did."

I frowned, thinking I understood a little—about how Anne Marie hadn't remarried, even though she'd apparently been attractive enough to—but not understanding completely. "Why?"

"Well, even though it was the sixties with the Civil Rights Movement and Women's Liberation in full swing, this was and still is deep country. An independent, attractive, strong-willed woman who didn't need a strapping young man to survive? Folks all over were slow to take to the idea, I suppose, and even more so here."

"So. Uh. Did you?"

He snorted, grinning again. "Boy. You are way past the age of misdirection. Well," he grinned wider, leaning forward on the kitchen table, "to answer your burning adolescent curiosity, no. The thought never crossed my mind, which is strange. She was an attractive, strong...almost mesmerizing woman. And on some level, I knew that. But this was also a woman who had fed me lunches, patched up my scrapes and cuts on my knees and elbows, sewed up and patched the knees on my jeans so I wouldn't get in trouble for rough-housing when I got home. And I could've very easily been her son-in-law. And we talked, Kevin, as a mother and son would've talked, for so many hours, at this table. So no. Never. But I'm afraid people probably did talk. Human nature, I suppose."

"Oh." I nodded slowly, though something bugged me, still. "Why haven't you ever talked about her, then?"

Dad shrugged and maybe even winced, slightly. "Your Mom tolerated her while we dated and for awhile after we got married, but I don't think she ever really understood how important our relationship was. She tolerated it, though...until you were about two or three years old. Think she got tired of the whole thing, even though she never really came out and said it. It was just something I sensed. So I slowly stopped coming around."

"Why didn't Mom want you to come here anymore? She didn't think that..."

He chuckled and waved a hand. "No. I don't think so. I do think, however, that to your mom, Anne Marie was a link to a part of my past that excluded her, even though Allie had long since moved overseas to London and settled down with a family of her own. And, considering that your mom grew up here too, went to the same high school as us and remembered seeing me with Allie all the time I think it made her a little uncomfortable, thinking how things *could've* been. Anne Marie was a perpetual reminder of that. Do you understand?"

I shook my head slowly. "Yeah. A little. I guess. Mom wasn't jealous, exactly...just sorta...creeped out?"

He grinned. "That works. Anyway, little by little, I stopped coming by until I was only visiting every few months and then only for an hour or so. And Anne Marie never said a bad word, or hinted that she was upset in the slightest. I think she knew and understood, and besides, if there was ever a woman who wasn't afraid of being on her own, it was Anne Marie La Pierre."

I let myself look around a little, and the shock wasn't nearly as bad as I'd expected. It had settled in, I think, the truth of this house being so abandoned, so ruined...but it was almost like I had double-vision: one second, I saw the ruined husk of a house we sat in now; the next, a warm, glowing, friendly place full of life and love.

"Dad...it feels like...I've been here, before. When I first saw the house, rode up to it, I felt like...I knew exactly what the house looked like on the inside and everything."

He smiled softly. "Well, you have been inside, a few times. Your Mom offered me an unconscious concession, I think, as I stopped visiting Anne Marie so much. A few Christmas Eves I brought you over here to have cookies or Anne Marie's Christmas fudge, and to visit a while. You especially liked cozying up to the wood stove that used to be here," he nodded over his shoulder, to the stripped and bare room behind him.

"That's why," I whispered, again not trusting my voice, "why I like hanging out in the den downstairs so much in the winter, isn't it? Our wood stove."

He smiled and shrugged, clasping his hands before him. "Maybe. Who knows? Anyway, we did that right up until you were five, the night we..."

He took a deep breath.

Pressed his lips together, tightly.

Sighed and said, looking away, "The Christmas Eve we found her after she'd had a stroke."

And then suddenly a memory hit me, so hard and fast it almost hurt, of going to see that nice lady in that warm house and how excited I was because of the cookies and fudge this lady always made for Christmas but how disappointed I was when we got there to find her lying on her face and sleeping on the kitchen floor and she'd dropped a plate of cookies all over and now they were ruined and couldn't be eaten and Daddy tried to wake her up but couldn't and had to call someone to get her and Mommy to get me and I'd almost cried because it was so scary and I didn't even get any fudge or cookies...

I blinked and swallowed, my spit and throat tasting sour. "I remember a little, now. Sorta. She was lying on the floor and I thought she was sleeping."

Dad nodded wearily, looking tired and worn. "She'd had a stroke and passed out. Doctors never figured why, really. She was in good shape for her age, didn't smoke or drink. Anyway, she recovered enough of herself to realize she couldn't take care of all this anymore. Which must've been so hard for someone like her. With Allie pretty established in London—though she did come back and visit when it first happened—it was decided that I'd accept power of attorney for Anne Marie."

"What's that?"

"I means I had the authority to make all future medical decisions for her in case she couldn't. Also, her lawyer put her land and holdings into a Trust—sort of an account, I guess you could say—and made me the custodian of that Trust." He held up the keys and jingled them. "That's why I have the keys."

"I don't remember anything else about her."

He nodded slowly, looking sad, regretful. "She slipped into dementia pretty quickly after the stroke. Things got...messy. I visited her when I could, but toward the end..." He shook his head. "I didn't ever want you to see her like that. And I'm not sure if she even knew who I was anymore."

"If she couldn't stay here, where'd she live?"

"At the Webb County Assisted Living Home. Until this morning, that is."

He looked at me, eyes bright, shining, his expression serious, again. "What time did you say you first came down here?"

I swallowed, my throat suddenly dry and thick. I remembered the time, in black digital numbers on my blue Transformers watch. "11:30," I rasped.

He nodded once, slowly. "That call I took in the garage, when you came back? That was someone from the Home, calling to tell me that Anne Marie passed away in her sleep at 11:30 this morning."

Silence.

Absolute silence, save the slight creaking of our chairs, and the whispering of the wind through some cracks upstairs, somewhere.

I stared at Dad.

His face blank, waiting, eyes shining. I shook my head, tried to say something and couldn't...and looked past him.

At that empty...and very clean, as if brand-new...Coke bottle sitting on the kitchen counter, sitting there as if someone had just finished it. And the words came from me, slipping out slow, sure and clear. "She...she told me to tell you she wasn't mad. Even though you didn't show up. That she wasn't mad and could never be mad, and that...you're a good boy. That you'd always be a good boy."

More silence.

And I kept staring at that Coke bottle, until I heard Dad cough. But when I looked at him, my Dad *wasn't* crying. He wasn't. But his allergies must've been acting up in that damp house, the way he kept sniffling and wiping his eyes with his palms.

9.

WHEN DAD AND I got back into his truck, all buckled up and ready to leave, the radio flipped on abruptly in a burst of static. This wasn't so surprising, in itself. The truck wasn't that old but the radio had gotten twitchy over the past year or so because of a loose wire somewhere. It had a habit of flipping on and off at random, and we were all used to that.

But as that hissing static resolved, I heard a tune I recognized, a tune I knew, and I shivered, remembering *her* whistling it while she cooked the best burger I've ever eaten…

"…*down in the hollow…playin a new game…*"

I turned and looked at Dad, my eyes nearly popping, jaw hanging open.

"…*with you, my brown eyed girl…do you remember when…*"

I swallowed and nodded at the radio. "That. She…she was whistling that while she cooked…"

He smiled, looking sadder…and, in a way, more at peace than I'd ever seen him…and he whispered, "She always did. It was her favorite song."

"Dad…" I shook my head, unable to tear my eyes away from the radio, belting out that song so loud and clear and beautiful, "what…what happened? *How* did it…"

He grabbed my shoulder and squeezed.

I looked at him and this time, his smile stretched from ear to ear. "I dunno. But sometimes, the *How* isn't important. Just that it *did.*"

He ruffled my hair, turned, put the truck into gear and we drove home to the tune of that beautiful song.

10.

DAD AND I never spoke again about that day. And I never did tell him where I got the vintage 1960s 7UP bottle that soon after appeared on my "stuff shelf" (alongside stock cars, Transformer and Star Wars models, scattered arrowheads, an old harmonica given to me by Grandpa Ellison, a die-cast metal Millennium Falcon, chunks of sparkling basalt from the railroad tracks, and all the other bits and pieces of the world that only boys find valuable). Though I'm certain he saw that bottle often, he never asked where it came from. I think he just knew.

The very next day, riding out to the Commons to meet Corey (I'd called him that night, claiming a slipped bike chain), I bumped my ten-speed over the tracks and kept going, my gaze straight ahead, on the road before me.

Because honestly? I was done with big mysteries of the universe I couldn't explain, and I wanted to get lost in something I understood: basketball. And that's what I did for the next several weeks. Woke up, did my chores, rode down Bassler Road to the Commons straightaway without even the slightest glance to the side and played basketball with Corey until I could barely stand. Then, I'd somehow ride (mostly coast) home again.

And slowly over the passing weeks I forgot about that road and its house. Or maybe desperately ignored it is a better way of putting it. Maybe that seems strange or downright impossible, that I could *ignore* something like that, that I could will myself to forget that day and that road leading to that house in the woods, where I impossibly ate a hamburger and drank a soda with Anne Marie La Pierre at the same time she was dying in a nursing home.

But regardless, I did forget about it. I rode by that spot on Bassler Road, just past the tracks, every single day of the week, Monday through Friday, and never once looked for that road. Family trips, three-on-three basketball tournaments, camp-outs and fishing took up my Saturdays; Sundays we attended church in the opposite direction, over in Booneville.

Also, the summer of 1990 proved eventful, all by itself. I played my first year of varsity summer basketball over at the Utica YMCA, spent my first week away from home at Golden Valley Basketball Camp, just outside town, got that kiss I mentioned (that's a whole different story), logged countless hours camping and tramping through *safe* woods we *knew*, and I spent many of the too-hot afternoons down in our cool basement reading.

So, I guess—weird as it sounds—enough other things happened that summer that I just kinda forgot about that house and Anne Marie La Pierre.

Or maybe *made* myself forget. Even with that vintage, 1960s 7UP bottle—clear, pristine, looking like it had just rolled down a conveyor belt at a 7UP bottling plant—sitting on my "stuff shelf." I just let that day sink down under all the average things a busy fifteen-year-old boy does over the summer. Hard to believe, I know, but there it is.

Until one day, the middle of August.

It was Friday, late morning, August 15. I was biking down Bassler Road, a whole summer of memories and excursions behind me, heading toward my last day of one-on-one summer basketball with Corey at the Commons (pre-season football practice was starting up the following week) when something made me squeeze those brakes and come to a hissing stop on Bassler Road's gravelly shoulder—after I'd bumped across the railroad tracks. When I turned and looked across the road, I think that, deep inside, I knew what I'd find.

The opening to that abandoned road in the woods, cleared of brush, looking like it had been open all summer. And to its left, a log cabin mailbox, with a newspaper sticking out.

And I know now (as I think I suspected then) that I'd so readily forgotten about that road, that house and what I'd seen there because it had closed itself off to me for the rest of the summer. How else could I have ridden by that spot almost every day and ignored it, had it actually been open? There was simply no way.

But there it was.

On that last free day of summer vacation.

And there was never any question in my mind.

I turned my bike, pedaled across Bassler Road and bumped off it, onto that road, and down toward Anne Marie La Pierre's house.

II.

THE HOUSE LOOKED as it had the first time I'd seen it. EXACTLY the same. Not abandoned, rotten or leaning, not boarded up with a sagging porch and a peeling, moldy exterior, but more in suspension, as if waiting, poised for something.

For me.

The rust-colored swing set stood tall, rigid and proud at the edge of the property where I'd seen it before, its swings hanging still. The vintage pickup truck—sitting on full and new black tires, window glass whole—parked before a sturdy garage.

I didn't knock on the front door.

Knowing, somehow, that it'd be unlocked. Also knowing that after my first visit I was not only welcome and had permission to enter...but that in some strange, weird way...I belonged here.

Just like Dad.

So I turned the knob, opened the door and quietly let myself in. I went straight to the kitchen, once again, not looking into the living room or up those steep stairs to the second floor.

She was sitting at the kitchen table. Looking exactly as before, not a bit different. Black hair shot through with a few strands of white-gray, looking neither older nor younger, perpetually middle-aged.

But in a way, she did look different. In her expression, in her unfocused eyes, staring out the dining room's sliding glass doors (also not boarded up). Her face, slack and loose, as if she'd fallen asleep with her eyes open. Sitting up, hands folded limply on that yellowed-ivory table-top. A glance behind her showed me a plate with two uneaten, recently cooked hamburgers—those remaining from the batch she'd cooked that day I'd first come here—and an empty Coke bottle standing next to them.

I coughed, clearing my throat.

Nothing.

"Ma'am?" I whispered, stepping forward, the floor creaking beneath my foot as I reached out and clutched the back of the chair before me, as if for support, to keep me standing.

A twitch at the corner of her mouth, a flickering eyelid.

I cleared my throat more loudly and somehow, in a clear and steady voice said, "Anne Marie."

She shivered and blinked, as if waking from a deep sleep. She cracked her neck, looked at me and smile-frowned, her eyes bright and alive again, face aware and attentive once more. "Hey, kiddo. Sorry about that. Must've been day-dreaming. You forget something? You want another burger, after all?"

I opened my mouth and floundered, momentarily at a loss for words, my mind suddenly dizzy with all the thoughts I'd

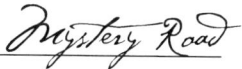

been avoiding all summer; thoughts about this house and its hidden-but-unhidden road, family secrets and the impossibility of *her.*

What could I say?

What *should* I say?

And why? At that moment, the sudden realization possessed me that I needed to be very careful in what I said, that I needed to be general and vague, that whatever was happening here...I was not to tell Anne Marie about it. I was to let her exist in whatever fashion she did and that was all.

"Thanks," I blurted out. I rushed on as she opened her mouth, looking even more confused. "I just wanted to say thanks again for the burger. That's all."

Still looking puzzled, she smiled warmly. "Well. You *have* been raised right, haven't you? That's nice of you, coming all the way back just for that. But you could of said that the next time, it's not like I'm going anywhere..."

She paused.

Her mouth hanging slightly open, mid-sentence.

And slowly, I think, understanding of a kind came to her. Her eyes took on a hooded, almost brooding look, and for a moment—an instant, only—my skin prickled with itching cold pimples, as something dark, desperate and maybe even dangerous flashed in those slate gray eyes.

She licked her lips and rasped, "What am I doing here? What is this place, *really?*"

Her voice vibrated with an almost cold menace. I stepped back instinctively, letting go of the chair. In my haste, I bumped my shoulder against the armoire behind me, stumbled and almost fell.

That and my most likely terrified expression must've cut through whatever dark emotions were surging through her, because Anne Marie's face immediately loosened, her eyes suddenly turning very distant, the dark fire in them fading. She sagged in her chair, bowed her head and covered her face with her hands. "Shit," she breathed once, the sobbing hitch of someone trying not to cry, "Shit."

And I stood there and she sat there for what seemed like forever because like the first time I'd been in that house, time had no meaning. But finally she sighed, straightened and began kneading her forehead with her fingertips, as if fighting off a migraine. From behind her hands, she said in a slightly muffled voice, "Okay, kid. Jig's up. Be honest and tell me God's truth. Where *are* we? What the hell *is* this...*place?*"

I stepped forward and swallowed, no longer afraid, but cautious. "Your home. It's...your home."

Another sigh, then a snort.

And Anne Marie La Pierre pushed away from the table and stood. She hugged herself and shivered, casting a suspicious glance around the dining room, into the kitchen. "No. It's not. It's not my home. I don't live here anymore, haven't since..."

She turned slowly and faced me, confusion in her eyes. Her mouth tightened and she said, "I was somewhere else. Somewhere else for a really long time, somewhere that hurt me, in my head, every day. Then I fell asleep, finally, and..."

She looked out the sliding glass doors. "An I woke up here. I was somewhere else, fell asleep, and woke up here. An at first I thought it was my home...but it's not. It isn't. I want it to be, really bad, but..."

She looked at me, bright and alive eyes meeting my gaze. "But it's not. I know that, deep down. Even if I don't want to."

Her expression softened somewhat, as did her eyes. Something shifted in them and she shivered again, hugging herself as she said, "And you're Brian Ellison's kid. I can see it in your eyes. At first I though you were him, and then I could see you weren't..."

She rubbed her upper arms, as if feeling colder. "So," she whispered, "what happens now? Where do I go from here? Do I go? Or...is this...it?"

I shrugged, feeling useless and helplessly fifteen, out of my depth. "I dunno. I just don't."

She grunted, as if expecting nothing more. Looked around, nodding as she did, as if working herself up to take stock of the situation. "So I wonder," she mumbled as she glanced around, "how long it's going to take me to get this damn place straightened up."

And I saw the change come over her. Just like that, in a snap. She hugged herself again and rubbed her upper arms once more, then placed one hand on her hip, ran the other through her hair, and looked back at me—looking exactly as she had the first time I'd met her, as if nothing had ever happened, as if she didn't even remember what had been said not ten minutes ago. "Listen, kiddo...Kevin, right? I've got some work to do around here...but are you hungry, by any chance? Was going to cook some hamburgers for my daughter's boyfriend, who was coming over to split wood...but it doesn't look like he's gonna show. They're yours, if you want them. Didn't you say you were heading somewhere to play ball, anyway? Bet you could use the food."

I smiled, feeling a kind of profound sadness—and acceptance—that I wouldn't understand until someday Dad himself slipped gradually into dementia, slowly sinking into a fantasy world of delusion, one that was best accepted and understood and left well enough alone so he could enjoy some semblance of peace until his time came to move on.

Because it was the same with Anne Marie. A different kind of dementia, true. But even back then, as I nodded, accepted her offer, pulled out a chair at the kitchen table and sat, I realized, somehow, that this existence was best left undisturbed, that for now...until it was time for Anne Marie to move on, wherever she was bound for next...things were better this way.

Because she'd found a semblance of peace.

And sometimes, that's all you can hope for.

12.

AND AFTER THAT last hamburger with Anne Marie La Pierre, after she'd said goodbye, claiming she had "lots of work to do round here" (as if she hadn't already said that to me once) I walked my bike back up Bassler Road and stopped and stared at that log cabin mailbox and the newspaper protruding out of it.

Stared at it for what seemed like forever.

Back then, I'd been an avid fan of the *Twilight Zone*. Still am, and thanks to Netflix, I watch it on my iPad all the time. Anyway, that show holds a special place in my heart because in my formative years it served as my first introduction to speculative fiction that attempted to talk about *big things*, the kinds of things that left your head spinning for days afterward. Even as a fifteen-year-old, I'd seen almost every episode and had memorized almost all of them, having watched them on reruns countless times. Enough times to know, somehow, what I'd find if I pulled that newspaper out of the mailbox, unrolled it and looked at the date. Somehow, I knew what I'd see.

But I didn't do it.

I mounted my bike and left that road for the last time.

Because sometimes, you don't need to know how something happened.

Just that it did.

13.

SO I STOOD there next to that log cabin mailbox with the newspaper sticking out, staring down that road—looking smooth and freshly paved—as it ran parallel to the train tracks for about half a mile before winding off into the woods. I took a deep breath, wondering why, after all these years, I could see that road and its mailbox again.

I never visited Anne Marie La Pierre after that last time. Pre-season football practice started the following week and soon after, school. Homework every night built up on top of practice and with games every Saturday, very quickly—even more quickly than it had over the summer—Anne Marie La Pierre and her house at the end of that road faded to a vague, distant memory of a weird thing which had happened that I couldn't explain.

I wondered, standing next to that mailbox, what became of her. Wondered if it had been Anne Marie at all. Had it been a ghost? Her spirit or soul, trying to pass on one last message?

And because I was standing next to that mailbox and could see that road again, after so many years...

Was she there?

Standing before that stove, cooking those burgers as if no time had passed since I'd last seen her?

Even now, a part of me hopes what I'd seen in that house— and what might've been there waiting, the day Dad died—hadn't really been Anne Marie, her spirit, soul or whatever. I hope that it had only been a fragment, some sort of echo, some part of her that hadn't been able to let go of what she'd lost. I hope that most of what she'd been, the woman Dad had known, went on somewhere better.

But I wonder, now.

Because I'd first met Anne Marie La Pierre in that house at the end of that road the day she died. And there I was, standing next to that mailbox, looking down that road again, mere minutes before Dad would pass on, the same place Ann Marie did, at the assisted living home.

After several more seconds of staring, my cell phone warbled in my coat pocket. I pulled it out, flipped it open and answered it without bothering to check the number, recognizing my wife's ringtone.

"Hey. Is..."

"*Yes,*" she whispered, "*I think it's getting close. You near?*"

I stared down that road for just a beat longer. "Yeah. Be there in a few."

"*Good. Hurry. Think it's going to happen soon.*"

"Right."

I hung up the cell, closed it, stuck it into my pocket, got back into the car and I pulled away from that mailbox for the last time.

⟊ ⟊

And as I pause in writing this, staring at my collection of vintage soda bottles (the still pristine-looking 7UP bottle in particular) along the back row of my far more cluttered and impossibly more juvenile "stuff shelf" down in my office, I allow myself, very briefly, to ponder a point I've always shied around.

What was that, in that house? Because it certainly wasn't heaven. Had Anne Marie gone there—her, an echo of her, whatever—because a part of her hadn't been able to let go?

I can't help but wonder, after all these years, if an echo of Dad found himself there, also. If that was why I could see the mailbox again, the day he died. Maybe Anne Marie La Pierre hadn't been *stuck* there, after all...

Maybe she'd been waiting. Waiting for him. Waiting for a time when she wouldn't be alone anymore. And on the heels of that, there's another thought: I'd felt so welcome there. Like I belonged there. Someday, when I pass...

Will I join them?

But I made it home in time to say goodbye to my father. I fulfilled my final duty as a son. There's no last message to pass on. And because of that, maybe, just maybe...

Well.

Maybe.

A Night at
OLD
WEBB

KEVIN LUCIA

CEMETERY DANCE PUBLICATIONS

Baltimore

❖ 2022 ❖

Originally published - Apokrupha
July 24, 2015

Praise for *A Night at Old Webb*:

"*A Night at Old Webb* is an intimate tale of youth, wonder, attraction, and exploration of mystical places. Blurring the lines between memoir and fiction, it's an unsettlingly sweet and sad story about friends, new and old, standing around being young together.
— Mercedes M. Yardley, author of *Darling*

Arcane Delights
Main Street
Clifton Heights
Saturday

"SO WE DID it. We got this place up and running." Cassie Tillman smiles as she stirs her chicken and broccoli with a pair of chopsticks. "Gotta admit, when you first hired me and showed me what was left here after that flood, I didn't think it was possible..."

She lifts her full chopsticks, chews and swallows, and waves around the store's back room. "But here we are. Two months open and chugging right along."

Cassie carefully shifts her feet—propped up on the big metal desk used mostly for this—so as not to disturb a stack of books. Digging chopsticks into her plastic take-out container, she grins. "Of course, you couldn't have done it without me."

Not nearly as refined nor as sophisticated as her, I spear a hunk of spicy shrimp with a fork. Smiling, I lift the morsel and salute her with it. "How well I know. Which is why the assistant manager's position is still open."

Cassie swallows another mouthful and shakes her head. "Sorry, boss. You know I…"

"…only work part-time. Part-time at three different jobs. Why I don't know. Because you don't want to be tied down. Or something."

I eat the shrimp and gesture at her with the fork. "Just so long as you know…"

"…the position's always open." Cassie smiles again. "Yeah, I get it. You've mentioned it a few times. Doubt I'll ever take you up on it, but if I decide to, you'll be the first to know."

I nod, knowing that's the best I can expect from her right now. Hyperbole aside, Cassie Tillman has been highly instrumental in getting my Dad's old store—now *my* store—up and running. Not only is she a hard, smart worker, she's offered some much-needed levity along the way, without ever overstepping her bounds. Her only informality is the occasional *boss*, which, coming from her, doesn't sound like the slight some might mistake it for.

Regardless, she more than deserves the assistant manager's position I keep dangling before her. If she ever decides to give up her oddly vagabond employment situation (she works two other part-time jobs besides this, as a waitress at The Skylark Diner and a nurse's aide at Webb County Assisted Living) and expresses interest in the position, it'll be hers in a heartbeat.

Though I can't deny how much comfort she provided Dad as his aide at the Home. He passed away in the grip of Alzheimer's and dementia a year ago, and she did everything possible to make his last days bearable. He didn't recognize any of us by then or know where he was or what was happening, but Cassie managed to establish a rapport with him. I'll always be thankful for that. If she wants to work three part-time jobs at once, more power to her. Especially if she helps all her patients like she did my Dad.

To distract my thoughts from Dad's passing (which, quite honestly, I still haven't dealt with completely), I glance around the store's back room while Cassie and I eat in silence. To my satisfaction, it looks exactly as it did when Dad ran it: barely organized chaos. Shelves built into the walls are stuffed full of books accumulated from library book sales, yard sales, rummage sales, discards from the local high school libraries, estate sales, and books donated from across Webb County. This big metal desk sitting in the center of the room is used mostly for newly acquired books that haven't been sorted yet, and for Cassie and me to rest our feet on during lunch breaks.

Against the back wall stand two empty bookshelves, made recently in case we need more space. Made by Cassie, of all people. Over the past two months I've learned that in addition to her three part-time jobs she's also a part-time, self-taught, self-employed carpenter who makes everything from classic Adirondack lounge chairs to picnic tables. She sells the bulk of her wares anonymously on Ebay and at out-of-town craft fairs. Her surprising hobby only serves to strengthen her strange charm.

Next to the door leading out front are two bins of battered paperbacks so beat-up I can't possibly charge for them. They trickle into the store in boxes of donations. I rotate those bins up front as "freebies" throughout the week. Patrons who take them probably never read them and eventually throw them away, which is probably what I should do, but I have this little quirk: I can't stand the thought of throwing books away. When I was still teaching high school English I brought home a box of discarded books every other month (much to my wife's chagrin) when the librarian stacked them on a table in the teachers' lounge. And I didn't even necessarily want to read them. I just couldn't stand the thought of them thrown into the recycling bin.

Digging back into my lunch, I think of how well we've exceeded my expectations. I'd mentally prepared myself for a shortfall the first few months until word got around we'd reopened. However, much to my surprise we've run a tidy little profit.

Our success can be attributed to how Dad ran Arcane Delights. He catered to all literary tastes. He was active in the community; hosting a variety of events: poetry readings, creative writing groups, children's story hour every Saturday morning, guest readers from out of town. He celebrated World Book Day and All Hallows Read, giving away free books for each, and he coordinated Scholastic Book Fairs at both Clifton Heights and All Saints.

People came from all over Webb County to shop here. He'd been active online with an email newsletter and a Facebook Page, and he sold stock through a number of online vendors. When Arcane Delights closed, many folks felt as if they'd lost a close friend or a dear member of the family.

When word traveled I'd inherited the store and was planning on re-opening, the response to our request for donated books proved generous beyond our wildest expectations. Dad had made provisions in his will for start-up funds should I choose to run the store upon his death, but he hadn't accounted for the inventory lost in the flooding. My initial estimates of how much it'd cost to obtain enough stock to re-open left very little margin for error.

We issued a call for book donations locally and on the internet. Almost immediately donations poured in. From families and libraries, publishers, other bookstores and individual authors. Several establishments even donated rare and hard to find volumes to bolster our Amazon and Ebay listings. It didn't take long to fill the shelves, creating the need for Cassie's hand-made bookcases.

This show of support has greatly eased my new-store-owner jitters. Abby (my wife) has supported me since the day I decided to quit teaching and take over the store. Never once has she expressed any doubt we'd stay afloat financially. She also maintains (only half-kidding, I think) I've been a lot easier to live with now that I'm not a grinding gear in the idiot machine of standardized high school education.

I'd be lying, however if I didn't admit some low-level anxiety about the coming months. The rent on Main Street isn't exorbitant, but it's not cheap either. I wonder what will happen when the glow of our reopening wears off, or if our online sales die out. What happens if we need to dip into our reserves to start paying the utility bills? Or if I need to start pulling funds from personal finances? I don't worry excessively about these things, but it wouldn't be truthful to pretend I don't mull over them occasionally.

Other aspects of this store occupy my thoughts, also. There's something different about this place. An odd vibe. Something in the air. I don't know if Dad ever sensed it. If he did, he never mentioned it. The sensation isn't necessarily unpleasant. I don't feel menaced or threatened. More like…observed. Even when working alone, I feel something hovering just beyond my senses, as if someone has ducked around the corner of the shelves to another row, or slipped out into the back room.

Of course no one is ever there. And I know it's probably just my imagination (which has always been overactive, leading me to many "odd" experiences over the years). But I often wonder if this sensation helped speed along Dad's descent into his Alzheimer's and dementia. Then, of course, I begin worrying about my own mental faculties, which never leads anywhere good.

Another bit of weirdness is the strange donation I received shortly before opening the store. A box full of old cloth-bound literary texts, both classic and obscure, what looks like a diary written in several different languages, an esoteric planting guide called *The Way of Ah-Tzenul,* and several black, leather-bound journals. The latter contains handwritten stories about life here in Clifton Heights. Written by whom, I don't know. The stories in the one I've read are far too fantastical to be true, despite an eerie verisimilitude making you want to believe they are. I haven't read the stories in the other journals yet, and haven't decided what to do with them once I have. For now, they're in the box they came in, at home in my office. They're never far from my thoughts, however.

All things considered, however, our first two months have passed much more smoothly than I ever thought they would. Even considering my worries about the store's financial future, its odd vibe and those strange stories in that journal, I'm happier and far more relaxed than I've been for quite some time.

Swallowing her last bite of lunch, Cassie looks as if something has just occurred to her. "Hey, before I forget. Martha Wilkins called while you were working on the website." A mischievous light twinkles in her eye. "She wants to know if any new Mills & Boon romances have arrived. Think she needs a new fix."

I cringed. "Thanks. I *was* enjoying this."

"I live to serve."

I shake my head, setting my box of spicy shrimp on the desk to open the top drawer. "Think I put the most recent inventory in here."

"Think you did? Don't you have a filing cabinet for those sorts of things?"

I snort as I dig through old inventories, pens, boxes of paper-clips and packing slips. "Or something. I'm pretty sure I put that list in here, though."

"What if it's not there?"

"Then it's probably in the middle drawer. Or the bottom drawer. Or out front under the counter." I look up and shrug. "Or maybe at home in my office. One of those places. I'm sure it'll turn up."

Cassie smiles and runs a hand through her purple-tinted black hair (purple *this* week). "Like I said, boss. Couldn't run this place without me."

Calmly pushing aside worries about my spotty memory and the Alzheimer's that very well might run in my family (tech-nically I'm too young to experience symptoms yet, but not unsurprisingly, that offers little comfort), I offer Cassie a game smile. "Don't I know it."

The middle drawer proves to be empty. The third drawer, however, turns the trick. The most recent inventory is right on top. "Ha! Told you it was here."

"There or maybe five other places."

I waggle a finger at her, shooting her a mock-stern look. "Be nice to your elder, young miss. Someday you'll be old and spotty like me. THEN you'll wish you'd been nicer."

"You better be nice to me. Especially since I'll probably be changing your bedpan in a few years."

I grimace. "There's a pleasant thought. Now I don't feel like eating dinner, either." I'm about to close the bottom drawer when I notice a sealed package I don't remember seeing when I stuffed the inventory list in there. Of course, considering I didn't exactly remember where I'd put said list, not remembering the package wasn't necessarily a big deal.

"Huh. That's weird."

"What's up?"

"A package. Looks thin. Like it might have a picture book in it, or something."

I pull the package out, heft it a few times. It's about the length and width of a picture book, or maybe a notebook of some kind. Pressing the package along its edge, I can feel something like spiral binding. Probably a notebook.

Cassie looks at the package with a thoughtful expression. "Huh. Doesn't look like a bound book. Maybe an ARC from a publisher?"

We get advance reading copies—usually for review purposes—in the mail occasionally, though I'm not sure why. Seeing as how I can't legally sell them, I wait until the publish date is far past, then dump them in the freebie bins. I heft the package again. "If it is an ARC, it's probably for a novella. Awfully light. Let me see the mailing address..."

I flip the package over to read the mailing address. At first, the words don't seem to make sense. Or maybe my brain just doesn't want them to make sense. On a second pass, however, the address reads all too clear, and an eerie wonder fills me. "It's...it's addressed to me. But to my address when I lived in Binghamton and was teaching at Seton Catholic, about ten years ago. And it's from..."

I scan the return address again, look up at Cassie and say, my voice sounding very far away, "It's from my father."

Cassie's eyes widen slightly. "Wow. Wonder what it is?"

I shake my head, looking back at the package, as if reading the address a second time will offer a clue. "I have no idea."

Instantly Cassie becomes all business. This is one of her strongest points. She intuitively knows when to get serious. "Listen, whatever it is…it's probably personal. If you want to take off for a while and check it out, I can mind the store until you come back."

I wait for a slight chill to run down my spine…but it never comes. Yes, this most likely is personal. But I don't sense anything secret about it. In fact, though I'd be hard pressed to tell you why I feel so, I sense whatever is in this package is meant to be shared.

I shake my head. "No…it's fine." I look up at Cassie and smile bravely. "Let's check it out."

I rip the flap open and slide the package's contents onto the desk. Sure enough, it's a notebook. A spiral MEAD notebook, the kind I used in high school for notes, and…

The royal blue cover strikes resonant notes deep inside.

"Wow."

"What is it?"

"It's one of my old notebooks, back from when I was in high school."

Cassie leans forward, definitely interested but trying to maintain a respectful distance. "What's in it?"

I smile-grimace, feeling my cheeks warm. "Stories, mostly. I wrote them a lot when I was in high school. In blue notebooks only, to keep them straight from my school notebooks. Must've accidently left this one behind when I went to college. Thought I'd taken them all with me."

"So you wanted to be a writer when you were a kid."

I nod. "Yeah. Dad sold about ten or eleven short stories in college. A small publisher released them in a collection right after he married Mom. It did okay, and he wanted to write more...but he didn't. Mom never told him no, exactly, but she wasn't very keen on the idea of him writing, from what little I've gathered over the years. And because she wasn't keen on the idea of Dad writing..."

"...she wasn't keen on the idea of you writing," Cassie finished. "Or, because she wasn't keen on it, you never shared your writing with anyone."

I nod. "The second one, yeah." Of course, what Cassie doesn't know is that part of the reason I quit teaching to take over the store was to try and free up time to finally start writing. It was one of the reasons why Abby supported the idea so strongly. She's been gently nagging me for years to start writing, citing Dad's short-lived career as something to avoid.

I shifted the package and heard something rustle inside. "Something still in here." I set the notebook on the desk and plucked a sheet of paper from the packaging. Flipping it over, I see it's a letter from Dad, dated about ten years ago, right after Mom passed away.

I hold up the letter to Cassie. "It's from my Dad." Before she can say anything, I flip it over and start reading.

"'Kevin— I was re-arranging the attic when I came across this in a box of your high school things. I hope you don't mind, but I've taken the liberty of reading it. There's a strong voice here, son. And I'm not just saying that because I'm your Dad. I'd always wondered if you'd done any writing of your own, also wondering—all respect to her, God rest her soul—if you hid it because of your Mother. Understandable, given her misgivings about my writing career.'

"'I hope you'll pardon my boldness, but I'm sending this to you with a plea: if you still write, if you even think of writing, don't *think* about it any longer. Your Mother loved and cared for me, and not a day goes by I don't miss her. But not a day goes by without me wishing I'd been more insistent on pursuing my writing. I could be wrong, but I sense in Abby someone who'd support your dream, if indeed it's still yours. And I know maybe you might not feel comfortable talking to me about these matters, but I'd love to discuss what you've written here. Again, I apologize if I've overstepped my bounds, but given the fate of my own writing career, I hope you'll understand. Love, Dad.'"

Silence.

Cassie waited respectfully, reluctant to intrude upon the moment, which is good. I'm moved by Dad's words on a fundamental level, and I don't trust myself to speak just yet. Instead, I lay the letter down, pick up the blue notebook and flip to the first page, only to be surprised once again, because on top is written: *A Night at Old Webb*.

"Holy shit."

"What?"

I hold up the notebook, my hand shaking slightly, a part of me almost believing this is a dream I'd wake up from, or that if I show too much emotion, the notebook will disappear into thin air. "I'd thought this one was long gone. Looked for it a few times and could never find it. Figured I'd just lost it somewhere among my moves."

"What's it about?"

I pause, wondering how I can possibly put into words the experience I'd recorded—in a very amateurish way—on these pages, the odd occurrences that took place the summer after my senior year in high school. Which should be easy for me, seeing as how I experienced my share of odd occurrences as a teenager. Even so, I opt for the simplest answer I can think of.

I shrug. "It's about...a girl."

Cassie grins. "Isn't it always?" As an afterthought, she adds in a more somber tone, "Wait. Is this something I should hear?"

"I don't see why not. Nothing really happened between Michelle and me. And I've told this story to Abby. In fact, that was one of the times I dug through my other old blue notebooks, looking for this one, when I wanted her to hear the story."

I meet Cassie's steady gaze. "No reason why you shouldn't hear it."

I admit feeling nervous, however. I haven't read these words in nearly twenty years. I don't exactly remember what they say.

"So." Cassie waves at me, "you going to read it or not?"

I look down at the notebook, open in my lap. "How about this? I'm not going to read it word for word." I smile at Cassie, still feeling a little embarrassed. "My Dad's praises notwithstanding, I wrote this when I was nineteen. And, if I remember my writing style from back then, I scribbled and crossed out stuff a lot. But I'll use it as a guide, and tell you the whole story. Sound good?"

"Works for me, boss." Cassie settles into her chair, re-adjusting her feet, as if sitting at the foot of a campfire. "Fire away."

"The first thing you need to understand before I tell this story is that…"

1.

THE FIRST THING you need to understand before I tell this story is how abandoned places have always called to me. I'm not sure why. Something about them intrigues me. Buildings once full of people, left forlorn and empty. I can't help but think of all those who once walked through their halls, slept in their beds, ate at their tables and called them home or work, wondering if traces or echoes of their passing somehow seeped into the walls and floors of the places they once inhabited. It's a well-worn cliché by now: houses, schools, hospitals, warehouses, churches (any place occupied by people) are like sponges, soaking up decades' worth of energies, both positive and negative.

It's why a well-told haunted house story still hums with such resonance. Something primal inside us wonders how much our homes remember their previous inhabitants. It's why kids are forever breaking into boarded up buildings. A derelict warehouse screams: "people once worked here!" and that scream is like an irresistible siren call to those of us too curious for own good.

It's why Clifton Heights kids make annual pilgrimages to Bassler House, or spend summer afternoons poking around the long-deserted shanty-village up in the hills behind Raedeker Park Zoo, or on Halloween Night try to sneak into the partially burned nondenominational Church of the Abiding Light on Gates Street. It's why intrepid (foolish?) people explore the ruins of Centralia, Pennsylvania (despite the still-burning underground coal mines) or, more locally, the abandoned town of Tahuwas, just forty-five minutes north of here. There are those of us who are, for one reason or another, taken with the desire to explore long-forgotten places once teeming with people, now filled only with dust and memories.

Old Webb High was one of those places, though how much of its allure came from its abandonment rather than its seclusion from adult eyes is anybody's guess. Twenty years ago, if you drove down Main Street and took a left onto Route 7, about five miles away from town you'd find it: Webb County Grade School. At one time it served kids living in both Clifton Heights and Old Forge. But the school districts were re-zoned in the early 70's. Most of the school's population was transferred to Clifton Heights Elementary. Since the Town of Webb School (located in Old Forge) was K-12, around 1971 or 72 the county decided to close Old Webb because its enrollment had dropped too low. The remaining numbers were easily transferred to Old Forge.

Nothing was ever done with the old building. A few years ago I did some research via Google. A few halfhearted attempts were made to turn the school into a retirement center, a residential home (first for disabled veterans, then for neglected youth) and a community recreational building. Jarred Simmons, the hotshot young Realtor back then, had also once floated the idea of turning it into an income-based apartment complex.

For one reason or another none of the ideas stuck. So in the Fall of 1992 the Town of Webb finally demolished the old school. Empty by then for nearly twenty years, the place had been falling apart. It had become something of a safety hazard, and also a regular party spot. Local teens had found several avenues of entry over the years, turning the old school into a clandestine meeting place for midnight jams and, believe it or not, romantic or at the very least illicit encounters.

I'm not ashamed to say my friends and I logged our time in "Old Webb." Like rooting around Bassler House, exploring the littered halls of Old Webb had become a rite of adolescent passage. My friends and I spent countless hours roaming there (always during the day), sharing stories about the tortured spirits of former students haunting those halls.

After we turned seventeen, of course, we visited Old Webb for different reasons: summer parties late Saturday nights. I don't mind admitting I drank my first beers and smoked my first cigarettes there (the latter of which didn't take).

I also had my first encounter with a girl on one of those Saturday nights, though it surely pales in comparison to the others Old Webb saw over the years. I still don't know what to make of my experience, or the events leading up to it. I can't exactly call Michelle Titchner my "first love" because I honestly didn't know her well enough. And after the summer of 1992, I never saw her again.

But she made a lasting impact. She was the first girl I'd ever talked to. Sure, I'd spoken to girls before and considered several of them casual friends. But something happened between Michelle and I which transcended any previous relationship I'd had with any girl prior. A sharing—for lack of a better term—passed between us. I can't call Michelle my first love, but I can say she became the standard I measured all girls against, and no one ever measured, up until I met Abby.

When email and the Internet became commonplace I tried to track Michelle down. I'd had no idea what I might possibly say to her, of course. By then—heading to grad school—I was savvy enough to know what little we'd shared wasn't enough to pick up again. I suppose I just wanted to see how she was doing, and to thank her for…well, thank her for spending what little time she did with me.

I did find information about Michelle Titchner, but nothing I hadn't already known. Nor did I find any way of contacting her. Of course, I'd half expected I wouldn't. Even if there had been a way to contact her, maybe it's for the best I couldn't. Some memories are best left untouched, lest some of the gold-tinged nostalgia get rubbed off, exposing tarnished brass beneath.

Besides, wherever Michelle Titchner is, I'd like to think she knows how thankful I am. She wouldn't say it, if course. She'd just offer me the quiet, knowing smile I nearly fell in love with that summer.

2.

TODAY I MARVEL at how often we slipped into Old Webb the last summer it stood on Route 7. Word had spread of its impending destruction and it seemed as if everyone who'd ever crashed there wanted to visit one last time.

I'm not naive enough, however, to imagine we evaded the authorities through our own cleverness. A lot of it simply had to do with Old Webb's location. Too far away from the State Police barracks in Woodgate, it didn't warrant any notice from them. Outside Clifton Heights' limits, it was also technically out of Sheriff Beckmore's jurisdiction, which, of course, didn't necessarily mean much either. Given Beckmore's ponderous disposition (from what I recall) Old Webb could've sat next to the police station and we probably still would've gotten away with our late night soirees.

Of course, Old Webb was part of Webb County, therefore falling under the jurisdiction of the Webb County Police.

It probably made a difference that Mitch Higgins (All County Quarterback three years running), son of County Sheriff Gerald Higgins, was a regular at the Old Webb parties.

It also probably helped that we never got up to anything really bad when we gathered at Old Webb. Sure, some folks occasionally drank too much, and I already mentioned the romantic encounters. Also, I'm not naive enough to believe no one ever indulged in the occasional joint, or back in the darker corners of Old Webb, something a bit more illicit. I never indulged nor saw anyone indulging in the harder stuff and neither did my friends, but of course that doesn't mean it never happened.

To be brutally honest, over the years I'm sure a few of those romantic encounters occurred under duress, or perhaps— shamefully—under force. But when my friends and I hung out at Old Webb, we protected our own. I remember one night in particular when some kid from Indian Lake tried to get Lizzy Tillman in a bad place. (Was she related to you, by the way? Oh. Your aunt.) Anyway, she shouted, we came running, and the kid was lucky to escape with his face intact.

Also, I'd like to think we exhibited a bit more common sense in those days. Kids have always been a little bent, of course. Teenagers even more so. There's always going to be those wild ones who run the razor's edge a little harder than the rest, or those who, for some reason or other, have a faulty conscience.

But I'd like to think we were smarter. More careful. We didn't get up to some of the crazier things I see in the news today (which makes me sound old, I know). We hung out, had a few beers, got a little loud and had a good time. I think the authorities knew this, and maybe offered us some slack because of it.

By the time my friends and I joined the scene, sneaking into Old Webb had become easy. Earlier explorers had to resort to boosting each other through broken windows around back of the school. Eventually folks got bolder and started leaving the front and side doors propped open with cinder-blocks. Since its closing, the wilderness had grown in behind and around Old Webb, effectively hiding those points of entry.

What happened to the front doors, however, proved to be a "perfect storm," in a sense. Back when Old Webb was still alive and kicking, administrators had planted two maple trees and some rhododendron bushes on either side of the main entrance. After its closing, those trees and bushes grew unchecked. They shielded the front door from the road's view, forming a leafy wall completely concealing the front entrance. Any car driving by—even at slow speeds—would never see the front doors past the foliage. The place appeared closed up and secure.

Duck under the maples' branches and you found something reminiscent of Peter Pan or some other fairy tale. A pocket where nothing had grown for twenty years. Under those maple branches, Old Webb's threshold and front doors were completely clear. Over the summers the front doors were always left propped open, a gateway to Saturday night freedom, safe and secure behind its green wall. When fall hit and our camouflage started to thin, someone would always shut the front doors, leaving the side and back doors cracked open. No one much went out there during the other seasons. It was an unspoken rule: Old Webb was a summer place only.

In retrospect, it's easy to see how someone in authority must've been giving us a blind eye. Back then, however, I suppose we simply thought we *were* that clever.

Past the front doors was the main lobby where the front office used to be. A hall led to the gymnasium, Saturday night's main destination. During the day, younger kids explored all of Old Webb's nooks and crannies. If I remember correctly, everyone avoided the basement, though. It was pitch black and crowded with desks, chairs and other pieces of furniture.

At night, older teens and recent graduates congregated in the gymnasium. We met in there for practical reasons. It was located in the back of the building away from the road and the trees had crowded in close to Old Webb over the years, shielding the gym's narrow, rectangular windows. Most practical of all, the gymnasium was an easily lit, wide-open space. Plenty of room to spread out and relax. Dozens of chairs and desks had been dragged into the gym over the years, arranged into small clusters where folks drank and talked the night away. Someone had jimmied the athletic supplies closet open and dragged out wrestling mats and high jump pits, arranging them in the corners, creating lounge spaces.

Back in the seventies lots of those old gyms had tile flooring instead of wood. Old Webb had been one of them. Because of this, a few old barrels had been dragged into the gym for use as makeshift fireplaces. We were really careful, however, always keeping the fires low, making sure they were out when we left. It never got cold in there anyway. Mostly we wanted fire more for burgers and hot dogs than for warmth.

I'm not going to pretend our gatherings at Old Webb held any mystical significance. Basically, for twenty years or so, kids sneaked into Old Webb on summer Saturday nights to hang out, drink, roast burgers or hot dogs and grope in the shadows. Every town has a place the kids flock to avoid parental supervision. Old Webb was ours.

Even so we managed to make it uniquely "ours." One example: the graffiti. As you can expect, two decades' worth of graffiti accumulated on the walls of Old Webb's gymnasium. Alongside the predictable teenage profanities existed personal expressions of hope, sadness and melancholy. Also, among the graffiti was some of the most striking pieces of art I've ever seen. Everyone's favorite was a mural taking up a whole wall, of the solar system from the moon's perspective, looking over the swollen curve of a glowing blue Earth. I've been to dozens of cities over the years and seen many stunning pieces of graffiti art in tunnels, on underpasses, and on the sides of trains, but I've yet to see anything better than the Old Webb Universe. No one knew who painted it, either. Seemed like it had always been there.

Word of Old Webb traveled the teenage grapevine over the years, bringing in folks from as far away as Indian Lake, Lake George and Woodgate. The "regulars" attended schools all across and outside Webb County. Encountering new people we'd never seen before turned into a weekly occurrence. I can't count how often one of us would ask on the way there, "Wonder who'll show up tonight?"

That's why I didn't think twice when Michelle Titchner came the first summer night of 1992. With all the new people coming and going every year, I'm sure I assumed she attended either Old Forge, Inlet, Eagle Bay or Tawahus High.

I remember when I finally did notice her. My friends and I were lounging around the wrestling mats. Sipping from our beers and eating the hot dogs we'd roasted. Chatting about nothing and everything at once. I don't remember what we talked about, at all. Whatever it was seems trivial, now, compared to my first sight of Michelle Titchner.

"Hey," I said abruptly, interrupting Fitzy telling us some story about this girl he'd met at a nightclub in Utica, "who's *that*?"

Everyone fell silent and turned, following my gaze. They, likewise, seemed struck by Michelle's presence. Myself, I'll never forget my initial sighting. It's superseded in my mind only by the sight of Abby walking down the aisle on our wedding day.

She was standing with a few folks next to one of the barrel fires. I can be honest in saying I don't remember much about what she wore. Maybe it's me—or maybe it was Webb County and the Adirondacks in general—but thinking back, the clothing styles of the early nineties seems bland. Like tapioca pudding. Or maybe back then (like now), I had no fashion sense, because for me jeans and a t-shirt mostly comprised the entirety of my wardrobe.

No, what I remember most about Michelle is her long, black hair. Maybe it's only flight of fancy or simple nostalgia, but I could swear it reached down to the middle of her back. Raven black, thick, lustrous, wavy—which is an important distinction. In the early nineties "big hair" was still hanging on. I'd never been a fan of that particular eighties quirk. Michelle's hair wasn't big. It flowed down in waves of loose curls. The kind a guy wants to bury his face in.

Also, the way she stood. Relaxed, one hand in her pocket, the other holding a bottle of beer with the loosest nonchalance. It spoke of someone easy in their skin, someone content with who they were. Though I've always considered myself reasonably well-adjusted I don't think I've ever felt a similar level of confidence.

She was tall. Nearly as tall as me. She didn't look like a basketball player or an athlete, but she moved with a certain kind of grace. I suppose she owed this largely to her confident posture.

And while my friends unabashedly ogled her, before I was aware of my actions, the kid who sat quietly in the back of the classroom and preferred to slide through life unnoticed stood and walked over to her. To this day I've never been able to account for this spasm of boldness. In high school I was the nice guy who didn't talk much. Unless I was on the basketball court, I felt more comfortable remaining in the background. Back then my chief goal was to draw as little attention to myself as possible. Most of the time, I achieved that with flying colors. Between my small group of comrades and the basketball team, I had enough friends. I didn't much feel the need to talk to anyone else. And like a lot high school guys, I was secretly scared to death of acting like an idiot in front of girls.

I still have no idea what prompted me to ditch my best friends in the middle of a conversation to approach the most striking girl I'd ever seen. A stranger, to boot. Call it a rare moment of teenage bravery. Or, perhaps I sensed how different Michelle was; somehow knowing an honest and unpretentious approach wouldn't be rewarded with rejection.

Hell, call it Fate.

Maybe we were meant to encounter each other and both of us knew it. Whatever you want to call it, or however you want to label it, the normally shy basketball player who did all his talking on the court closed the distance between him and a striking girl in less than thirty steps.

Sensing my presence, she immediately shifted her gaze to meet mine and smiled softly. With little to-do, I stuck my hand out and said, "Hey. Kevin Ellison. Don't think I've seen you here before. You go to school around here?"

I have no idea what prompted me to speak so boldly. It may seem strange, but though I taught high school English for ten years, I've never liked to talk much in social situations, especially to strangers. In the classroom I assumed a certain persona. I was "Mr. Ellison." After ten years of teaching that persona carried weight, making it easy to play a role.

But in civilian life I have been and always will be merely "Kevin," who is still that teenager scared to death of acting like an idiot. A guy who, deep down, remembers a stuttering problem that plagued him in first and second grade. A guy who is always afraid that, despite years of speech therapy, his stuttering will return at a moment's notice.

(You tell anyone about that, Cassie, and you're fired.)

Anyway, how did I speak to Michelle Titchner so easily? I think a lot of it had to do with the natural calm radiating from her. Something about the set of her shoulders. The relaxed way she held her beer. Her entire posture spoke of a laid back, easy-going individual.

I sensed she was merely passing time. Someone was speaking near her, but not to her. She seemed to be listening because she had nothing else better to do at the moment. In fact, to this day, I think that was the deciding factor. If at the last moment someone had asked her a direct question and she had responded with interest, I'm sure I would've veered off for the coolers to get another beer I didn't really want.

However, no one spoke directly to her. She appeared politely detached, merely observing the conversation rather than taking part in it, which made me feel much more relaxed.

She accepted my handshake with no pretense, her smile widening. Her smooth, soft skin held the faintest warmth. An icy thrill ran through me. I'm still surprised I didn't jump at her touch.

"Michelle Titchner. And no, I don't attend school around here. Not anymore, anyway. Just visiting for the summer."

I raised my eyebrows. "College, then. Webb Community or Utica. Syracuse, Le Moyne?"

She offered me a cross between a wince and a smile. "Mmm, no. College wasn't for me. Sorta just hanging out right now."

"I get it. Cool." Which sounded like the lamest thing ever. Somehow I avoided wilting in terminal embarrassment and plunged ahead. "So. How'd you hear about Old Webb?"

She smiled, like she was enjoying a joke both of us were in on. "Well, c'mon. Everyone knows Old Webb. Common knowledge. I've been here before, just haven't been in a while." Her smile faded, expression growing somber. "Besides. I heard the news. About what's happening in the fall."

It was an unconscious thing, but somewhere in the middle of our blossoming conversation she'd left the group around the barrel fire and had meandered away aimlessly, me following. It suddenly occurred to me, here I was: Mr. Shy wandering off with perhaps the prettiest girl I'd ever known, and I wasn't terrified.

I grunted. "Yeah. County has finally decided to do her in. Knocking her down, bulldozing her under. I'm glad I'll be away at college. Kinda sucks. Would hate to be around when it happens."

Away from the barrel fire, her face fell into shadow. Another good thing about meeting in the gymnasium—at the back of the building—we could bring in plenty of Coleman lanterns and no one would see us from the road. Still, there was no way to light up the whole gym, so pockets of shadows lingered here and there. We were wandering through one of those when the shadows brought out something I hadn't noticed before: her vibrant green eyes, which glowed with gentle warmth.

She gave me an amused smile, bright eyes wide. "That's interesting. You calling Old Webb 'her.' Is it a she, you think? Why 'her'?"

I shrugged. "Dunno. It's like a calling a ship or a plane or a car 'her,' I guess. A gesture of...respect, maybe?" Again another lame answer, but all I could do was smile, slightly abashed, and shake my head. "I have no idea."

She smiled back, offering a wink. "It's okay. I think you're right. Old Webb is a 'she.' And yeah, I haven't been out here for a while but when I heard about how they were planning on tearing her down," she glanced at me in emphasis, smiling wider, "I had to come. Figured I'd spend the summer here, seeing as it's...it's gonna be the last, I guess."

"Ah. I see. So you're not here for the fine dining, beverages, and illuminating conversation? That, and of course," I gestured at everyone either lounging in chairs and on wrestling mats, or clustered around lanterns and barrel fires, "all the excitement."

There were many things she could've said to this, but she simply offered a small, pleased smile, one I'd get used to and cherish soon enough. "Oh, I don't know. Conversation's been illuminating so far."

I managed to chuckle without gagging, glad we were wandering in the shadows, so she couldn't see the red I felt burning on my cheeks.

She took a sip of beer and, as if sensing my embarrassment, launched right back into our conversation, perhaps hoping to stave off an awkward silence. She tilted her head toward the front hall. "So. You ever explore the deep, dark recesses of Old Webb at night?"

I pantomimed a shudder not entirely feigned. "No thanks. I'd like to think I'm not a coward, but even with a flashlight or lantern, it's pitch black out there in those halls. Especially downstairs."

She grinned. "C'mon. You mean to tell me a good-looking guy like you has never gone 'exploring' Old Webb with...someone like me? A girl to impress, maybe?"

Amazingly enough the insinuation didn't embarrass me nearly as much as it normally would've. The idea actually made me laugh. "Nooo. No thanks. See, my friends and I used to wander the halls out there in the day—it's dark enough in some places even then—and though I'm pretty sure Old Webb's structurally sound, there's desks and chairs and all sorts of crap all over the place. Old wires hanging down from the ceiling and all. Groping with someone out in those halls at night? Not exactly my idea of romantic."

She nodded; giving me a look of grudging respect. "All right. Fair enough. And you do seem the romantic type. Holding the door open, buying flowers and candy and Hallmark cards on three month anniversaries, laying jackets over puddles, the whole bit."

I looked down, mostly to cover the red I felt must be painted all over my face, also feeling insanely pleased inside. "C'mon. How can you tell all that? You just met me. Known me a whole five minutes."

By then we'd traveled across the entire gym to the doorway leading out into Old Webb's dark halls. She turned and leaned back against the wall, giving me the up and down, appraising me. "Five minutes is all I need. All anyone needs."

"Really."

"Sure. I've got this theory. If you're observant, pay attention and are a good listener, five minutes is all you need to figure someone out, enough time to tell whether someone's worth your effort. That's why everyone always says first impressions are so important, right?"

"Five minutes. Really. You size someone up and judge them in only five minutes."

She held up a finger, oddly like a lecturing teacher. "Not judge. Evaluate is a better word. You pay attention to body language, mannerisms, speech, a person's aura..."

Here I smiled a little bit, trying to be polite and not laugh. "Their aura."

"Yep. How they carry themselves, right? If they're overly aggressive, too passive, stubborn, or kind." She tilted her head and locked gazes with me, brilliant green eyes shining. "If you pay attention you can figure everything out in about five minutes."

"Yeah, but why do people always say first impressions can be misleading?"

She arched her eyebrows. "People who say that don't pay good enough attention. For example, let's pay attention to *you*."

I blinked, embarrassed but still, crazily enough, pleased. "Me?"

She nodded, smiling her smile again. "Sure. I had you pegged in five minutes. First of all, you're not as shy as you obviously think you are."

I opened my mouth—a bit like a fish freshly hauled ashore, I'm afraid—coughed slightly, then managed, "How...how do you know I'm..."

She grinned, her green eyes dancing. "Because. It's in your eyes. This whole time, you've had this slightly glazed 'holy shit I'm talking to a girl' look in your eyes, and yet...check it out." She waved at me. "Here you are chatting me up, chilling out, not trying any corny come-on lines, totally relaxed. I think you perceive yourself as being shy and withdrawn, which is why you don't talk to girls much. But here you are. Talking to a girl. Interested enough to ditch your friends, whom I'm guessing are your best friends, too."

My scalp tingled slightly. This was amazing, bordering on spooky. "How do you know they're my best friends?"

She shrugged. "You looked relaxed when you were hanging with them. Could tell by your body language. Completely at ease, no pretension. You feel accepted by them, and you don't feel like you've got anything to prove. Plus, they let you alone when you came over to me. Only real friends would do that. Bunch of macho assholes would've been cat-calling you by now, giving you a hard time. But they're best friends, so they're letting you be. For now. Tomorrow they'll rag your ass. Because best friends save that stuff for private."

I crossed my arms, more intrigued than embarrassed. "Wow. All in five minutes, huh? And...you were watching me? The whole time before I came over?"

She smiled gently, sipped from her beer, swallowed, and said, "Maybe."

I opened my mouth—doing the fish-thing again—but she quickly added, "Also, you pay attention to people. You're interested in what they have to say. Even though you came over to chat up a girl you found attractive..."

I snorted, amused (and amazed) at her boldness. "Right. Because you're so hot and all."

She shrugged again. "It is what it is. Anyway..."

I couldn't help but laugh at her bald-faced confidence. Thankfully, she responded with a chuckle of her own as she continued. "Anyway. This whole time you've looked me straight in the eyes while we talked." She tapped two fingers under her eyes. "Your focus has been right here. Says a lot about a person."

"Not really. I mean...you've got really pretty eyes."

Holy shit.

Did I really just say that?

But it must've been the right thing to say, because she acted a bit taken aback by it. "You think so?"

"Well, yeah. Your eyes are this really bright...green I've never seen before. I mean, maybe I'm not such a great guy all focused on people and what they have to say. Maybe I just think your eyes are really pretty."

Again: Holy. Shit.

Seriously?

She smiled, holding up her finger like a teacher gently catching a student at an important point. "But see, of everything you could've been staring at, of all the things you could've found attractive..."

"Because there's so much," I offered, amazed now at my daring, which was growing in leaps and bounds by the minute, "because you're so hot and all."

She smiled and tilted her head, as if reluctantly conceding the point of her hotness. "Anyway, you're attracted by my eyes. Not my body, like a macho asshole would've been. You were drawn to my eyes."

A sensation I'd never before known took hold of me. I sipped my beer, took a step closer—noting she didn't cringe away, just looked up at me, chin tilted upward slightly—and I managed to say without the slightest hitch, "They say eyes are the windows to the soul. Maybe you've got a really pretty soul."

A slow grin spread. "Now that, my friend, is a line. But it's a damn good one."

In an instant my panache dissolved. "Good thing, because I've used up my repertoire for talking to pretty girls. Got nothing left, I'm afraid."

She did something, then, which sent a jolt through me more powerful than anything I'd ever felt before. She smiled and lightly placed her hand on my chest. "And see, you're honest. You're completely willing to admit my hotness has got you tongue-tied…"

I laughed again.

"…and instead of covering with macho bullshit, you admit it. That's honest, and refreshing."

I smirked a little. "Too bad I'm not as modest as you."

She laughed, eyes glinting as she removed her hand from my chest and ran it through long, black hair I desperately wanted to touch. "And you can poke fun without being a dick. A precious commodity, trust me." She shrugged. "See? Five minutes."

"No way. I haven't been timing it or anything, but that had to have taken at least seven minutes. Maybe eight."

She shrugged again. "Give or take. But who's counting?"

I sipped from my beer and swallowed. "Not me. I'm a book guy. And writing. I avoid numbers and counting whenever possible."

"And see? You're funny, too."

"Only by accident, trust me."

She offered me possibly the sweetest, purest white-toothed smile I'd ever seen, before or since. "But that's when a person is funniest."

After several more minutes of banter, it couldn't be avoided any longer: the awkward lull in the conversation when both people have run out of things to say. I found myself leaning toward her, staring into her bright green eyes, also noticing her bright red lips, which, though still smiling, were also damp and glistening, and parted slightly.

All the signs screamed kiss her.

But I didn't.

After all these years, I remain convinced not kissing her was the best choice I could've made. It was a test, I believe, though I have no way of knowing for sure, nor exactly what it was a test of.

I stumbled back from that particular precipice the first night I met Michelle Titchner. I coughed slightly, stepped away and sipped from my beer before saying, "So. I've already used up all my wittiest quips. What do you like to do? I mean, I already sorta told you what I'm into, the reading and writing. What about you?"

She paused, thinking, and then said, "I like to talk. With people. No one really talks to each other, anymore. They talk at each other...but not *with* each other."

I shrugged. Suddenly, all the tension and awkwardness drained away. "So let's talk. Don't know if I'll have much to say, but I promise to nod in all the right places."

She gave me a smile which would've driven me insane with jealousy should she have offered it to anyone else. "Throw in an occasional 'Really? That's interesting!' and you've got a deal."

That's what we did for the rest of the night.

7.

"SO WHAT'S HER name?"

In a pleasant fog, I turned from the dark nightscape slipping past Gary McNamara's truck windows. "Hmm?"

Gary smiled mischievously, one step away from a good-natured leer. "Her name, dork. The girl you spotted halfway through the night. The one you ditched us for?"

I smiled (probably like a love-struck idiot) and shook my head. "Sorry. My mind's a little…" I wagged my hand away from my head, pantomiming a bird flying off.

"Yeah, I figured. As did everyone else, trust me. She must be something, pal-o mine, cause you got it bad. Which," he returned his gaze to the road, "is about time. Your commitment to basketball has been impressive and all, but you've needed a girlfriend for about two years."

I shook my head and gazed back out the window. "She's hardly my girlfriend. We just met. Plus…I think she's older than me. Said she doesn't go to school anymore and she's not in college, so she's probably *way* too old for me."

"And...does she have a name?"

"Michelle Titchner," I murmured, recalling in my mind's eye her long, thick black hair and sparking green eyes.

"Michelle Titchner."

A pause, and then: "Huh."

I glanced at Gary, who was still concentrating on the road. "What do you mean, 'huh?'"

He glanced at me, brow slightly furrowed, but he grinned and waved, "Nothing, man. Wow. You've really been bitten, haven't you?" Turning his attention back to the road, he continued. "I didn't mean anything. It just...feels like I've heard her name before. Michelle Titchner."

Now that he'd mentioned it, so had I. In fact, in retrospect, I think some voice had been whispering how familiar her name was in the back of my head from the moment she'd mentioned it. I'd pushed it aside because I wasn't sure if I really recognized her name, or if I wanted to recognize her name. Having someone else voice the same thing, however, strengthened the impression of having heard her name somewhere before.

"Huh. You're right. It does sound familiar. Don't know from where."

Gary's shrug was evident in his voice. "Maybe sports? She's kinda tall and lanky. Probably played basketball or volleyball or ran Track."

I frowned at him. "Lanky? Really? You think she's *lanky*?"

"What? She's tall and has long arms and legs. Lanky, dude."

"No way. Mark Bohynski is lanky. She is most definitely not lanky."

"So what is she?"

I thought for a moment, searching for the right word. Willowy wouldn't mean much to Gary; hell, I'd only seen it used in novels, never heard it used in real life. After a moment, I settled on the best words I could come up with. "Elegant. Graceful. Definitely not lanky."

Gary shook his head, smiling. "Elegant. This is what I get for hanging with a book nerd. Elegant."

"A book nerd who can dunk on your ass. Elegantly, I might add."

He snorted, offered me a sidelong grin. "Whatever. You. Got it. Bad."

I punched him lightly in the shoulder. "Naw. She's kinda hot and funny. We talked. That's all."

I turned back to the darkness, trying to ignore the slight twist in my guts whispering it was all a fluke and I'd never see her again. "That's all," I whispered.

⌇

I didn't realize how much I was mooning over the mysterious Michelle Titchner until Wednesday afternoon, when Corey Bainbridge and I were playing hoops at the Commons Trailer Park. Ten years ago the owners of the Commons put in a regulation-sized, full-court asphalt basketball court. I guess the plan had been to follow up with a playground, but for some reason those plans fell through, leaving only the basketball court.

No one ever played on it. I'm not sure why. The court was beautifully level and smooth, practically begging for players, but no one ever showed up. Maybe it was too far away from the school, where people (myself included) played every night of the week over the summer. Why travel to the edge of town to play on a nice enough asphalt court when all the real action was always in town at the high school?

For me, living on the town's outskirts, the Commons basketball court was only a bike ride away. Since I first discovered it the summer of my seventh grade year, I'd biked there daily over the summers to shoot around or work out with my best friend and teammate, Corey.

It was during my afternoon workout with Corey when I realized how preoccupied I'd become with a girl I'd only met once. Though things had felt normal Monday and Tuesday, nothing felt right that Wednesday. I'd drifted in a fog all day. Sleepwalked my way through chopping firewood in the morning, took forever to bike up to the Commons (I had my driver's license, but both cars were in use that day), and for two hours squaring off against Cory, I couldn't buy a basket. I felt slow, my legs heavy and my hands clumsy. I had fallen one-step behind Corey on nearly every play.

My last jump shot had just bricked off the front of the rim out of bounds. Corey checked the ball at the top of the key, but when I checked it back to him, he caught it and held it on his hip, asking, "Dude. You okay? You're like in space or something."

I frowned, pretending I didn't understand. Amazing how willing we are to engage in the futile efforts of self-deception. "What? I'm fine. Having an off day is all."

Corey raised his eyebrows, tossing the ball lightly from one hand to the other. "An off day. You call missing every jump shot and losing three games in a row by five or six points an 'off day?'" He shook his head. "I'm as confident as the next guy, but no way I'm beating you that bad. You're not here, Kev."

I grinned with false bravado. "Check-it, Nancy Boy. You're about to see the greatest comeback in the history of basketball since the '83 Celtics/Lakers series."

He rolled his eyes as I hunkered down into a defensive stance, rechecking the ball. I flipped the ball back to him, he rocked left, and I...

saw Michelle's bright green eyes

her flowing black hair, and her smile

...stood still as Corey exploded right, leaving me in the dust.

It was painfully apparent, no denying it after that. I was somewhere else. Corey had always been faster than me, but I'd had quick feet, I was long and—hell, lanky—and usually played better defense than that. I barely recovered and cut him off on the wing as he pulled back, eyes narrowing, shoulders set, preparing to launch one of his deadly accurate jump shots...

I totally swallowed it.

Hook, line and sinker.

Instead of gathering the ball in from his dribble and jacking a jumper in my face, he stutter-stepped and blew right by me. He coasted to the hoop and laid the ball off the metal backboard with a light metallic ping, followed by the hissing-snap of the ball popping through the net.

He grabbed the ball out of the net and stared at me. "Greatest comeback ever, huh?"

I settled at the top of the key and motioned him to the check me ball. "It's coming, baby. You wait. It's coming."

Corey shook his head but said nothing, checking me the ball. Three missed jump shots, a turnover, a botched lay-up and five straight buckets by Corey later and I'd lost every single game to him for the first time since we'd started working out together five years ago.

After his winning jump shot swished through the net, Corey smacked my shoulder on his way to retrieve the ball. "Like I said, mi amigo: In space. Out near Jupiter, man."

I chuckled, caught between amusement and unease. Back then, writing was merely a secret hobby I told no one about. Teaching high school English was a vague "career goal" to satisfy my guidance counselors. Basketball was my thing. Had been since fifth grade. Corey was good and fast and quick, his jump shots machine-like in their precision. He'd beaten me plenty of times before, but we usually split our wins and losses down the middle. He was right. I felt miles away from the court.

Because of her.

Michelle Titchner. A girl I'd met once. At an Old Webb party, of all things. Regardless of her lustrous black hair, burning green eyes and ethereal presence, thinking a girl could throw me off my game so bad…it was disconcerting, to say the least.

I trudged over to the grassy bank on the far end of the court, which sat in the shade provided by the tree line. Feeling as cumbersome as I'd played, I flopped onto my back and closed my eyes. Corey retrieved the ball, jogged over and sat next to me.

"Twitter-pated is the word, my friend. Twitter-pated. Bad."

I snorted, my eyes still closed. "Dude. Really? Bambi? What are we? Five years old?"

"Bambi is a timeless classic loved by all."

"This coming from the guy who cried when Bambi's mother got shot."

He grabbed his sports bottle from his backpack, nodded and added before taking a swig, "Also the same guy who laughed when ET died. A cinematic event you didn't take so lightly, my friend."

"Bite me."

"Only if you shower first, precious."

This brought a round of laughter. I loosened up inside, feeling better instantly. I trained year round—running and lifting weights when I wasn't playing—and I was due a bad game now and then. So what if I was a little preoccupied? At least it was over a girl as impressive and…as intriguing as Michelle.

As if sensing my thoughts, Corey fist-bumped my shoulder and said, "Don't worry about it. I didn't get a good look at her, but if she was half as hot as she seemed from where I sat, I totally get it. I'd be in a fog, too. Besides. You're Mr. Basketball. You deserve a little time off, right?"

Second time I'd heard that in less than a week. "Yeah. I suppose."

Corey sipped from his water bottle again. "So. Talk to her since then?"

The question took me aback. I shook my head, because no. How could I? I…

"Never got her number," I muttered with a sinking feeling in my gut, instantly knowing how lame I sounded, and what it probably meant.

Corey sputtered a little, wiped his mouth with the back of his hand and offered me an incredulous smile. "You spent the whole night talking to this girl and you didn't manage to get her number? How'd that happen?"

I glanced away, feeling embarrassed, as if somehow I'd violated some important "guy-code" titled: Always Get Her Number. Or at least try. Which I hadn't at all.

I shrugged, still staring at my feet. "I dunno. We talked the whole time, then we ended up walking to Gary's car, she said goodnight…"

I shrugged again, abashed, glancing at Corey sidelong. "I dunno. Never got it."

He appeared sympathetic, which made me feel worse. "Ah, dude. Hope you didn't get played. Maybe she's got a boyfriend. Hell, if she's a little older, a fiancé. Maybe she was slumming it and didn't want to give you her number so you wouldn't go screwing things up with her man."

Unable to help it, I bristled. "She didn't say anything about a boyfriend."

I nearly winced soon as those words left my mouth.

"Of course she wouldn't tell you. Didn't want to scare you off. Maybe she wanted to chill with someone other than her man, wanted to feel single again, so she crashed Old Web alone, and then you came along, chatting her up. She was more than happy to play along, and hey: maybe she dug you a little, too. Maybe her boyfriend's possessive or whatever, so she liked you and liked pretending you guys were working the mojo. But really, she was playing you. Probably didn't mean to hurt you or anything, but at the end of the night, she was going back to her man, no matter how cool you were."

He shrugged. "Sucks, man. But it happens all the time."

I looked away without saying anything because, of course, it was all very plausible. Even if I felt Michelle and I had connected on some deep level, Corey's explanation sounded credible. More than likely it had happened to plenty of guys, probably right there at Old Webb.

Stubborn, I shook my head. "I dunno."

Corey lurched to his feet and kicked mine. "C'mon. Stand me one more game, then we'll head into town and grab some subs at Dooley's. Sound good?"

I nodded slowly and stood. We stretched a bit, warmed back up, and shot for possession. Corey bricked his three.

Mine hit nothing but net.

It depressed me, in a way, that our little talk had blown my pleasant haze away. I didn't enjoy beating him nearly as much as usual. As much as I'd won, I felt like maybe I'd lost something a lot more precious inside.

4.

THOUGH COREY'S COLD dash of reality felt unpleasant at the time, it did serve to shake me out of the clouds and
back down to earth. The price was a slightly jaded view of my
encounter with Michelle, but I finished the week sharper, on my
toes, with a clearer head.

I finished my chores more quickly and efficiently the rest
of the week and hung out more with my friends, catching
the Wednesday Night Creature Feature at Raedeker Park—
THE MUMMY RETURNS—with Bill Ward. I went fishing with
Gary McNamara and Nate Slocum, picked blueberries at Mr.
Trung's blueberry patch with my sister on Thursday. I did all
the things I normally would. Corey's dose of reality took the
shine off things a little, but it also brought my feet back down
to the ground.

Next Saturday night, at Old Webb?

She didn't show.

Surprisingly I didn't feel too badly about it. A little bummed, maybe, but it seemed confirmation of Corey's theory. I decided to take the previous Saturday as it was: an enjoyable evening spent with someone unique, nothing more.

Having driven myself to Old Webb that night, I left early. I couldn't deny feeling a little let down, which did steal some of the usual fun.

5.

LIFE SETTLED DOWN nicely the following weeks. My disappointment at Michelle's no-show did linger for a few days, but mostly, I carried on as normal. I played hoops every day with Corey. I chopped firewood; hit the beach at Clifton Lake. I went hiking, fishing, and I played more basketball...all the usual things. In the face of this normality, Michelle Titchner faded into the background, although I'd be lying if I said her memory disappeared entirely.

I stayed away from Old Webb for several weeks, which helped. There were plenty of other things to do on Saturday nights: camping out, heading to Old Forge for fireworks, Five Mile Speedway with my Dad, Utica for the movies, and my classmates' graduation parties. I managed to keep busy. Of course, if I'd thought about it I would've realized I was avoiding Old Webb. Avoiding the reality of Michelle Titchner never showing up again, or worse, showing up with this theoretical "man" of hers.

I successfully stayed away from Old Webb for the bulk of July. Until the last Saturday, July 27th. That weekend was the Gus Macker, an annual three-on-three basketball tournament held in Norwich, about two hours downstate. For an entire weekend, Norwich became a basketball Mecca for players of all ages.

Unfortunately, we bowed out of the tournament early, losing two hard-fought games Saturday. For the first time in three years myself, Corey, Mike Fitzgerald and Micah Cassidy (a stand-out player from Old Forge High) wouldn't be playing Sunday. Someone floated the idea of a "consolation party" at Old Webb. Everyone voted on it unanimously, myself included.

Ironically enough, I didn't think of Michelle Titchner until we slipped through the tree-shrouded front doors of Old Webb and made our way to its lantern-lit gymnasium.

Soon as we entered the gym, I saw her. Like last time she was standing near a group of people clustered around a fire barrel. Sipping her beer, not really taking part in the conversation. I wasn't looking at her for more than a minute or two before she glanced in my direction, nodded and smiled her little smile and started toward me.

Gary must've seen this because I immediately felt his elbow nudge my side. Corey clapped my shoulder and whispered something like "she's all yours." I shrugged him off, turning toward her.

We met each other halfway. She smiled. "Hey."

I smiled in return, desperately hoping I didn't look like a moron. "Hey. Been awhile. Didn't see you last time I was here, then I got busy for a few weeks. You haven't been..?"

I snapped my mouth shut, worried I was not only rambling but also acting pathetically desperate, but she didn't notice. She shook her head. "I couldn't get away last couple weeks. Nothing personal, don't worry. Not like I was avoiding you or anything."

I chanced a grin of my own, once again feeling an uncharacteristic boldness rise in me. "So you weren't slumming or taking a break from your boyfriend or fiancé or..."

For one terrified moment I thought maybe she might be offended, but she laughed, eyes glowing with amusement. "Wow. Boy pulls no punches, comes out swinging. Let me guess." She nodded over my shoulder. "That's all your entourage has been saying since last time. 'She's probably got a boyfriend anyway, so forget about her.' Am I right?"

I glanced over at my friends, who were clustered around a small portable grill getting their usual hot dogs, beers already in hand. I glanced back to Michelle, chuckling. "They mean well. Worried I'm losing my head, getting all twitter-pated, and such."

She raised an eyebrow. "Wow again. Bambi. Double-cultural points for your friends. I figured their comments would've been more like: 'Dude! Don't be so pussy-whipped!'"

I laughed outright. "Well, actually, Fitzy did say that. The one with the red hair, last time? He's not here tonight."

She laughed also. "You have some interesting friends, Kevin Ellison."

Once again, the smile on my face must've made me look like an idiot kid on Christmas morning. "Good thing, because I'm not interesting at all. We balance out, I suppose."

She mock-scowled at me as we turned slightly and started meandering away. "Now, c'mon. A nineteen-year-old who's filled notebooks with short stories and poetry he won't let anyone read because he's going to college on a full basketball scholarship next year? Sounds interesting to me."

Once again I felt thankful for the dimness in Old Webb's gymnasium, because my cheeks felt hot with embarrassment.

Had I really told her all that stuff last time? About these blue spiral MEAD notebooks of mine?

I realized with a mild sense of shock I had (I must've, right?), which officially made her the first girl I'd ever told those things to. Stuffing my hands into pockets, I glanced down (stopping short of scuffing the floor with my toe), and muttered "Naw, that's not important. Just me messing around is all."

I forced myself to meet her gaze. "Writing is fun. I mean, I like to make stuff up, see the story in my head and all…but it'd be hard to make a career out of it, I guess."

Her gaze sharpened slightly. For the first time I thought maybe something harder lurked behind those beautiful green eyes. Not something malicious or mean, but intense. "Let me guess. You've gotten the whole 'do something practical' speech from your parents, right? Dad told you not to waste your time on pipe dreams like writing for a living?"

I meant to smile, trying to lighten the mood, but it felt more like a grimace. "Well. Yes, and no. I have gotten the 'do something practical' speech—mostly from Mom—but I've never said anything to Mom or Dad about my writing. I think Dad would dig it. He teaches English at All Saints. Over in Clifton Heights? He loves reading and writing as much as I do, so I think he'd understand why I like to write…"

Michelle nodded slowly, realization dawning in her eyes. "He tried to write, didn't he?" A pause, and then a gentle, "Did he fail?"

I shook my head. "Well, not really. I actually think failing completely would've been better. Then he could've put it out of his mind for good. No, he sold a handful of short stories during graduate school, right before landing his job at All Saints. After he got married, he sold the stories as a collection to a small publisher. He wanted to take a year off from teaching and really make a go of it. Write some more stories, maybe write a novel..."

"But..?"

I shrugged. "Mom wasn't into it, I don't think. I mean, don't get me wrong. I don't think she ever told Dad in so many words to quit writing. But I think Dad knew taking a year off to write wasn't going to fly. He landed the job at All Saints..."

Michelle nodded, her expression grim. "And he never wrote again."

"Nope. His collection sold well, though. He sold a few hundred copies. But that was it. Got too busy with school, grading papers, doing lesson plans, the usual teacher things. Plus...like I said. Don't think Mom ever forced him to quit, but because he knew she wasn't into it..."

"He didn't have the heart to go on," she finished for me. I glanced at her, surprised, because she sounded angry. Like she was taking it personally. "No offense," she added, "but that's bullshit."

I shrugged. "No offense taken. Mom and I don't exactly fight, but we don't really see eye to eye, either. She wasn't thrilled I got the basketball scholarship, believe it or not. She thinks I'm gonna grow these crazy dreams of playing pro ball someday."

Michelle smiled, her—anger?—fading. "Little does she know, it's far worse. Her son's grown crazy dreams about being a writer someday."

"Yeah. That would go over wonderfully, I'm sure."

She cuffed my shoulder. "Hey now. No self-pity. No offense to your mother, but you're not gonna let her kill your dream, like she did your Dad's."

I rubbed my shoulder and pretended to wince (but not completely; she had put some unexpected *oomph* behind her swing). "She didn't kill his dreams, really. More like starved them."

"Whatever." She waggled a finger in my face, scowl-grinning. "You're not going to let her do it to you. Understand?"

I chuckled, holding my hands up in surrender. "Sure. Whatever you say. Just don't hit me again."

"Depends. Promise you won't give up? You'll keep writing? Make sure to marry someone who nurtures your dreams instead of starving them?"

I stared at her for a moment—lost in those green eyes—marveling at her mature self-possession, intrigued by her sense of the world beyond herself. None of her rant had been a veiled suggestion she was the one to feed my dreams. It hadn't been a flirty gesture to win me over. She was genuinely adamant I keep writing.

Which of course only made me fall for her even harder.

I nodded, smiling in wonderment. "Yeah. I won't give up. Promise. First novel gets published; I'll dedicate it to you."

She waved. "Naw. Dedicate it to whomever helps get you through it." Her small smile crept back. She glanced at me sidelong. "However, a hat-tip at the end of your acknowledgments will do nicely."

I laughed, shaking my head. "You got it."

A moment of quiet followed, against the backdrop of other people talking and a boom box playing, ironically, "You Want It" by FAITH NO MORE. There was no awkwardness. It was a comfortable quiet, the kind usually existing between those who are so intimate they feel no pressure to fill the silence with chatter. Like many other things, I've only ever experienced this with one other woman besides Michelle: my wife, Abby.

After a few more minutes of this wandering around and chatting, she placed a hand on my shoulder, (which made my heart beat triple-time) and said, "Hey. Wanna see something cool? You ever explore the woods on the other side of the road?"

I peered at her, curious. "No. Why?"

She gripped my shoulder, eyes alive, excited. "It's…well, I'll be honest. It's kinda eerie. But kinda cool, and definitely not boring. You game?"

I remember feeling a little unsure for the first time since meeting Michelle. Part of it was the break in routine. Everyone visited Old Webb because of Old Webb. I'd never heard of anyone exploring the woods around it, or across the street. But also…

A special knowing glinted in Michelle's eyes.

As if she had access to secrets I'd never understand.

My journey through adolescence into adulthood was one of constant discovery. I learned many things growing up that completely altered my view of the world. I wasn't sure what Michelle wanted to show me in the woods across the street, but while most of me was intrigued, a smaller part of me felt…

Anxious?

Apprehensive?

Afraid?

To this day I'm grateful I repressed that cold feeling in my stomach, plastered on a brave smile and said, "Sure. I'm game." Perhaps it was only a small moment in the face of life's panorama, but like so many other small moments…

It changed so much.

6.

LUCKILY I'D BROUGHT a flashlight with me so we had light to leave by. Which was good, because I might've had a hard time walking without one, as excited and nervous as I was. Rationally, I knew it was unlikely Michelle was leading me across the road with amorous intentions. However, I was a nineteen-year-old guy, so part of me couldn't help but feel hopeful.

Another part of me—a much smaller one, but no less vocal—truly felt some anxiety. No one had ever mentioned anything worthwhile seeing across the road from Old Webb. Which begged the question: was Michelle leading me across the road because she had something to show me, or had she lied, and was leading me somewhere for something…else?

I suppose it's obvious I hadn't seen many slasher flicks as a high school student. If so, I might've been a little more suspicious of a girl I hardly knew leading me out into the night in a secluded part of the county to "show me something really cool."

Especially when she took my flashlight, saying, "I know where we're going, so this'll be easier."

Regardless, most of my unease faded as her free hand took mine, the simple contact of flesh against flesh soothing. We walked across Old Webb's moon-glimmering parking lot, our feet scuffing the cracked asphalt in the night's silence. At the time I didn't have the vocabulary to adequately describe the scene. If pressed, I probably would've offered something like "really pretty in an unreal sort of way."

From my vantage point today, (though my perspective is obviously tinged by nostalgia), I remember the dreamlike image of the yellow stripes running down Route 7, glowing under a full moon. Everything was cast with the faintest luminescence. The trees, the road, and the star-strewn sky. The deep quiet of the Adirondacks swelled around us and pressed in, dampening the faint strains of Guns 'n Roses' "November Rain" drifting from Old Webb behind us.

If pressed today?

Ethereal would be the word.

We stopped at the road's shoulder. Michelle shined my flashlight on a darker patch of woods on the opposite side. "See that," she whispered. "it leads to an access road. Most people miss it, because the trail-head is so overgrown."

I squinted. Sure enough, she was right: I could see a gap in the foliage. Looked like any "official" Adirondack trail-head you'd see in the Adirondacks, but without the blue, gold-edged sign telling you the trail's destination. "What's back there?"

"You'll see. Do you know what the land here was used for before Old Webb came along?" I shook my head, but I'm not sure she saw me, because she continued without a beat. "Believe it or not, it was a Bible camp. When the Town of Webb bought it in

1930, it built around the camp's dormitory and expanded it into Old Webb Elementary."

We crossed the road, our sneakers whispering against asphalt. Most of my anxiety had given away to intrigue. I don't care how old any guy is; exploring abandoned places always holds a special allure. "How do you know all this?"

I glanced at her, my breath nearly taken away. In the night, lit by the backwash of the flashlight, Michelle appeared to be otherworldly. Like a beautiful nymph from faerie realms.

Of course, that's more rose-tinged nostalgia for you. Back then, I probably thought to myself: "Wow. She's hot."

She offered her knowing smile. "I haf my vays," she whispered mischievously in an awful Euro-trash accent. I snorted, and she chuckled along with me.

On the other side of the road we ducked under low-hanging tree branches and past brush into a surprisingly clear, rutted path winding up into the forest. Clearly, at one time, vehicles of some kind—if only tractors—had driven up this road.

"This used to be a big part of daily life at the old Bible camp," Michelle whispered as we picked our way carefully up the old access road, the flashlight's splotch of white bobbing along the path before us. "It wasn't owned by the Bible camp, but the owner worked with the camp. After the Town bought the camp and built Old Webb, the owner of this plot worked with the school, offering special after-school riding sessions, weekend training, offering its premises for 4-H meetings for many years before the administrators decided to eliminate 'non-essential extra-curricular' programs and activities in the wake of educational 'reform.' Y'know what the worst part was? The owner of this place offered her continuing services for free but was still turned down because at the time, Old Webb's administrators were hot in pursuit of state funding through mandated, 'approved' curriculum and educational planning."

"Riding sessions? 4-H meetings?"

"Yep." We rounded a corner. She panned the flashlight back and forth across a clearing. "Check it out."

I'm not sure how many times in my teenage years I was actually rendered 'speechless,' but I can safely say I was that night. The access road opened into an old clearing inexorably being reclaimed by the surrounding woods and waist-high brush. An abandoned but oddly preserved cabin sat far back to our left.

In the middle of the clearing, the barest remnants of fencing could be discerned in the brush, and if you had a good imagination, you could fill in the blanks and trace the fencing around a small pasture. Back in the far right corner leaned what might've once been old horse-stables for maybe four or five horses (Corey's younger sister took lessons at Pleasant Hill, so I recognized the stables easily enough).

"A horse ranch," I whispered. "Those are stables back there."

Michelle nodded, smiling. "Yep. Imagine this entire pasture picked clean, and countless footpaths and trails for rides winding through the woods, and you'd have Shady Acres Horse Stables."

I glanced at her, raising an eyebrow. "Shady Acres, huh? Not exactly original."

She shrugged, sweeping my flashlight back and forth. "But it was *right*. Which is sometimes better than being original."

We passed the next few minutes in silence, making our way toward a section of fencing still standing upright. Any nervousness or anxiety I'd felt had faded in the face of a wondrous kind of...well, exultation; I guess you could call it. I was struck nearly dumb by the sight. It sounds contrived, but it was as if the moon had specifically chosen to shine down into the clearing, casting everything in its pale white glow, making everything ghostly, insubstantial. I firmly believed if I dared blink, everything would vanish.

We made our way toward a surviving section of old fencing. I gripped it, tested my weight against it, finding it surprisingly sturdy. I folded my arms on the top rung and leaned against it, gazing at a weed-filled, moon-fired pasture that had once played home to horses and their young riders.

(This, of course, is the part of the story you've probably been waiting for this whole time.)

Michelle sighed, leaned against me, slipping her arm around my waist, resting her head in the crook of my neck and shoulder.

I could feel the pulse of her breathing against my ribs. Her soft breath caressed my skin. A part of me soared inside. Remarkably, however, I mostly felt calm. At peace. Yeah, I was basically cuddling with an attractive girl out in the middle of the dark woods, but I don't remember consciously thinking anything. Nothing like, "Now's your chance, kiss her quick!" I was there with her, at that moment, which was more than enough.

After several minutes of a bliss, Michelle whispered against my neck, "I'm not slamming your Mom. Honest, I'm not. But you're not going to let her beat you. Are you?"

"No," I answered immediately, full of sudden, surprising conviction. "I'll find a way to keep writing. Dad never talks much about his own writing, but if he knew I was writing, too…I think he'd want me to keep it up."

She snuggled closer. I slipped my arm around her waist, pulling her tightly against me. "Good," she whispered, her warm breath sending chills across my skin. "When you give up something you love, when you stop fighting…you lose something, inside. And you're always haunted by it. Trust me."

"How do you know?"

She shrugged. I couldn't see her face, but I knew she was smiling her small little smile. "I just do."

We stood there for a while, holding each other silently, trying to preserve the moment in moonlit amber.

7.

EVENTUALLY THE NIGHT'S creeping chill overwhelmed our moment and we made our way back down the access path to Route 7. As we drew closer to the road, leaving abandoned Shady Acres behind; our conversation grew more mundane, rooted in everyday things. Though I don't remember telling her about the Gus Maker tournament the last time we talked, she asked how we fared and I told her. We chuckled about bad officiating and the unpredictable bounces a basketball sometimes takes. She proved remarkably knowledgeable on the subject, asking if I was excited about playing college basketball the following year at Webb Community College. I offered ambivalent answers, wondering (perhaps for the first time) how invested I was in basketball, anymore.

We crossed the road. Slipped back into Old Webb and ended the evening as we had before: chatting about nothing and everything. Corey finally found us, said he and the guys were heading out. Seeing as how they were my ride, and Michelle had made no mention of giving me one, I reluctantly gave in.

Michelle walked me to Corey's car, where we exchanged a far too causal "see you around," as if we'd just spent the night chatting about school gossip, rather than discussing my writing dreams. There was no goodbye kiss (not with the guys there), or even a hug, just a small squeeze of her hand and her knowing smile.

We drove off and I looked back, saw her watching us. As we rounded the bend, she turned and re-entered Old Webb, where I knew from past experience the party would continue for several more hours. I never once thought she was going back into Old Webb searching for another guy to hang on, though my friends joked (with no malice) about it. For the rest of the ride home, I was convinced she'd come tonight specifically to see me, and what she'd shown me in the ruins of Shady Acres - whatever it was she had shown me—had been for me, in particular.

To this day I still wish I'd made a greater effort to get her phone number. If she'd given it to me—if she'd *had* one to give me - it might've cleared up quite a few questions.

Because I never saw Michelle Titchner ever again.

8.

THE FOLLOWING WEEK, I felt...different. That's the only way I have of describing it. Following an urge I barely understood but had to obey, I called Corey and told him I was taking the week off from basketball. Told him I wanted to rest for a few days. I didn't know what was going on inside my head, but in retrospect, I think I now know: A part of me, hidden deep inside, had given up basketball.

Not completely, of course. And not immediately. I'd play for two more years at Webb Community. I'd enjoy it, and I would play well. But the week after seeing Michelle Titchner for the last time, something inside knew the time had come for basketball to fade, that the time had come for something else to take its place.

Back then I didn't think anything so concrete. I just knew I didn't want to play basketball for a while, maybe even a whole week. I wanted to write. So every day after my chores I borrowed the car and drove to Bassler Memorial Library where I hid at a table in the back and began my first halting attempts at writing this story, in this blue notebook. Of course, there were a few things I didn't know then, until Gary McNamara called me up the Saturday morning at the end of that week.

⌒⌒

"Hey. You busy?"

I cradled the phone between my ear and shoulder, scooped a spoonful of cereal in my mouth, chewed, swallowed and said, "Not really. Was thinking of fishing later, maybe. Depends on how hot it's supposed to be. What's up?"

"Can you swing by Old Webb?"

Something in his voice sent a mild shiver down my spine. A catch in his breath, maybe. Something in his tone. Of course, I'd spent the entire week trying to put into words this strange, weird thing between me and a girl I'd only met twice, and now here Gary was, asking me to meet him at the only place I'd ever seen this girl, but during the day. It occurred to me as an afterthought that I'd not wandered around Old Webb during the day since I was twelve or thirteen.

I slowly placed my bowl of cereal onto the counter, shifted the phone to my other ear, staring at nothing out the kitchen window, into our backyard. "Sure. Was thinking of fishing near there, anyway."

"Cool. See you in a bit."

"Right."

I hung the phone back up on the wall. Stood and stared out the kitchen window for several more minutes. Gary and I had always been okay friends, but we'd never done much on our own. Just him calling me was weird; and him wanting to meet me at Old Webb during the day, *alone*, was even weirder.

The feeling that had floated around me all week, a feeling of change, intensified. For the first in my life I felt unsure of what lay ahead. I realized with a mild sense of shock I enjoyed that uncertainty, which also frightened me a little, too.

9.

I PULLED BEHIND Old Webb and parked next to Gary's beat-up Isuzu pickup truck. He was waiting for me by the rear entrance, flashlight in hand. I parked, shut my Ford Escort off and got out, offering Gary a puzzled smile. "So what's up? We're kind of old for 'come see the cool gross thing I found,' aren't we?"

Gary smiled a little, but I could see it in his eyes. Something lingered there, a nervous energy seemingly all out of proportion with the situation. Also, his smile was brief, tight at the corners, like he was trying to smile and show how cool he was, show he wasn't...

Afraid.

I folded my arms, something strange and unbalanced—like I was sitting in the front car of a roller coaster teetering over the edge of its first drop—stirring in my stomach. It shocked me a little, again, to find the sensation not entirely unpleasant.

"Gary. Dude. What's going on?"

He licked his lips. "It sorta popped into my head, this morning. Don't know why, but it did. Remember how I said I thought I'd heard her last name before. Titchner?"

I nodded, a curious numbness creeping over my mind. I remembered because I'd thought the same thing, too.

"So I asked my Mom. And she…well…"

He gestured at the propped open back door with his flashlight. "Let's go check it out."

He ducked through the door. I followed; once again pursued by the thought everything in my life was about to change.

We walked down Old Webb's main hall, our sneakers scuffing against debris-strewn concrete. The building's immense emptiness pressed in around us. I couldn't deny feeling a little creeped out. I hadn't scouted around Old Webb's halls for a few years. Mostly, I only went on Saturday nights anymore, with twenty or so people hanging out in the gym, muted boom boxes playing in the background. I'd forgotten about the oppressive silence filling the halls when Old Webb was empty.

And as we made our way down the hall and past the gym to the other side of the building, Old Webb's strange air of hurried abandonment weighed upon me. The school hadn't been cleared out or stripped of useful furniture or appliances. It had seemingly been closed "as is." Classrooms not plundered by Saturday night guests still held rows of desks, some of them eerily straight and neat, monolithic teacher's desks and podiums looming before them. If it weren't for the graffiti on the walls, the litter strewn everywhere and the ceiling tiles piled on the floor in sodden clumps, you'd think a weird sort of

suspended animation had descended upon Old Webb, lock-
ing it in the same condition as the day it closed. Despite the
common knowledge Old Webb had been closed because of
"dropping enrollment," I couldn't repress the fantasy of something compelling the entire school population to abandon the
building en mass, never to return.

We turned right at an intersection. The hall stretched
onward, an endless, cavernous abyss. Despite myself, I wondered what kind of rodents or small animals hid in the darkness,
and felt glad for Gary's flashlight.

We walked only a few feet before Gary stopped so abruptly
I almost plowed into him. He didn't say anything, however, his
usually sarcastic air dampened by the weight of Old Webb's
emptiness.

We stood before a double door. I peered through the windows and saw a long counter. Rows of rectangular tables marked
the interior. Bookshelves ran along the walls, also standing in
rows on the room's far end.

The library.

"For some reason that girl's last name was bugging me this
morning," Gary whispered. "Don't know why. So I asked Mom.
Y'know she attended third grade here, before it closed? Anyway,
I asked her if she recognized 'Titchner' and she said...well."

He aimed the flashlight above the double doors.

I wanted to, didn't want to, and I looked anyway.

SOMETHING SOMETHING MEMORIAL LIBRARY.

I read it again, because for some reason the first part didn't
register. When I finally did see the name fully, I stared for several
more minutes, unable to pull together my thoughts.

MICHELLE TITCHNER MEMORIAL LIBRARY.

I opened my mouth.

Closed it.

Opened it again, but nothing came out. I'd read about moments of open-mouthed shock many times in stories, but until then I'd never thought it was something people actually did. Luckily, Gary kept right on talking.

"Mom said they got a big speech at the beginning of every school year, their first trip to the library. Back when this was a Bible Camp or something, there was a horse stable across the street. Up in the woods, called Shady Acres. Anyway, this lady—her name was Michelle Titchner—had wanted to work with horses her whole life, but back then I guess girls were supposed to get married and pop out kids, and that's all. Least-ways, around here that's the way it was. Only she said 'screw it' and did her own thing. Got disowned by her family but ended up owning her own little horse farm, Shady Acres. She lived there, too, in a little cabin or something, her whole life. After Town of Webb bought this and turned it into Old Webb..."

I sort of tuned Gary out for a bit.

I'd heard this part already, of course.

"...anyway, I guess when she passed, she left a lot of money to Old Webb. They renovated the library, renamed it the Michelle Titchner Memorial Library."

He stopped, abruptly falling into silence. We stood there and stared at MICHELLE TITCHNER MEMORIAL LIBRARY without speaking.

Finally, I swallowed and managed, "What...what does this mean?"

Silence.

Gary shook his head. "Hell if I know. Nothing. Probably a distant relation is all. Maybe she doesn't even know about this."

I nodded dumbly, knowing different, of course, having seen the remains of Shady Acres myself, having heard almost the same exact story from a girl named Michelle Titchner, who'd exhorted me to follow my writing dreams and not buckle under parental pressure to pursue something more "practical."

"Yeah," I rasped. "Probably. Gotta be."

There was nothing more to say. We stared a little longer, then turned and left. Gary decided—despite other plans—to join me fishing, which worked out because I always brought an extra pole. Apparently he hadn't wanted to spend the rest of the afternoon alone.

I felt the same way. Because if you have a chance for company, why would you want to be alone?

10.

I'D LIKE TO say I went to Old Webb one last time. I'd like to say I had the courage to attend one last Saturday gathering before its scheduled demolition in the fall, and I'd like to say I either saw Michelle Titchner one last time, or I visited the ruins of Shady Acres once more and felt some sort of resolution, some answer to the mystery.

But let's be honest. I was a nineteen-year-old kid confused about his future, tugged by the sport he'd played since fourth grade but also compelled by some new, strange desire to chase dreams through pen and paper. Confronted with so many choices about my future, as well as something I didn't understand in the MICHELLE TITCHNER MEMORIAL LIBRARY?

I pushed my questions away.

Buried the things I didn't understand and focused on what I did: basketball. With the first semester of college and pre-season practice looming, its familiar immediacy was comforting, far more preferable to thoughts of an uncertain future, cataclysmic changes, and the MICHELLE TITCHNER MEMORIAL LIBRARY.

I threw myself into my chores and then my afternoon work-outs with Corey. I ran and lifted weights with reckless abandon. I relentlessly prowled the asphalt courts of Old Forge and Inlet with Corey and my friends, playing hours of basketball. It served me well. I started as a freshman at Webb Community, played well enough to earn Freshman of the Year honors in our con-ference. And hey—I still enjoyed playing basketball fine, even if my passion for the game was slowly fading. But the truth?

I didn't pursue basketball so intensely the next two years because I loved it more than anything else. I buried myself in it so I wouldn't have to think about things I didn't understand and couldn't explain.

Which was fine with me.

I've thought about Michelle Titchner off and on over the years, focusing, of course, on the time we spent together, what she said to me, and our moment under the moon. Her arm around my waist, mine around hers, her head nestled on my shoulder. I relegated things like Shady Acres and the MICHELLE TITCHNER MEMORIAL LIBRARY to the locked box I believe we all carry deep in the primitive corners of our brains.

Michelle Titchner.

Who was she?

A ghost?

A distant relative of the Michelle Titchner of the MICHELLE TITCHNER MEMORIAL LIBRARY?

Why? Why me, why that summer of 1992?

Does it matter?

Even now, I'm amazed at how she managed to deflect or avoid any probing questions about herself or her background, where she lived, went to school, and her telephone number. A logical, rational assumption would be that she was an intensely private person sharing a moment she knew wouldn't last with someone she realized wasn't ready for the likes of her. Maybe the two names were completely coincidental.

Also, her dress, manner and speech fit right in with the rest of us. Sure, she acted a little wiser, and a little more "knowing" than her apparent age. She was an "old soul," as my grandfather was fond of saying. But she fit right in with the 1990's. Nothing stood out, no outdated mannerisms or sayings, no out-of-fashion clothing.

But if ghosts do exist, what would we know about them? How do you develop "rules" governing what the supernatural can or can't do? Who's to say a ghost—from a person who'd lived a fulfilling life, from a person who'd apparently died peacefully in their home—couldn't adapt themselves? Learn? Blend in as part of the crowd?

Especially if they were lonely and wanted someone to talk to. Especially if a place she'd dedicated so much of her life to was about to be bulldozed into the ground.

Couldn't she come say…goodbye?

In the end, I believe it doesn't matter. The only information I've ever found for Michelle Titchner was for the decades deceased horse ranch owner, the one to whom Old Webb dedicated its library years before I was born. However, I like to think that —living somewhere in the United States, or still lingering around what's left of Shady Acres—Michelle Titchner is happy we met and shares the same memories I do of those two nights.

I hope she knows—wherever or whatever she is—that I was finally ready for someone like her when I met Abby, and it was she who helped prepare me for meeting her.

And I hope that, somehow, someway, she's no longer lonely.

ARCANE DELIGHTS

I CAN HONESTLY say that in the short time I've known her, never once has Cassie been rendered speechless. Until now. A hushed silence falls after I finish my story, in which Cassie sits and stares at me, blinking. She opens her mouth to speak, thinks better of it and closes her mouth, looking deeply thoughtful, her brow furrowed. I notice idly that at some point during the story she slid her feet off the desk, and is now leaning forward, as if she's been hanging on my every word.

Another minute passes.

And another.

Cassie finally shakes her head and says, "Boss. Wow. And you didn't want anyone knowing you wrote stories when you were a kid. I mean. WOW."

Oddly enough, now that the story's been told, I no longer feel embarrassed or nervous. Mostly, I feel at peace. I haven't revisited my encounter with Michelle Titchner since I first wrote it down twenty years ago, and I wonder how much of it has been simmering in the back of my mind without me even knowing it.

I smile and shrug. "Well, keep in mind I didn't read you the exact words I wrote back then, just sort of ad-libbed based on what I remember, and what was written down. The actual writing itself is pretty simplistic."

Cassie gave me a look I can't quite define, almost reproachful and kind at the same time. "Yeah, but the way you tell it now...damn. Write that down, boss. Write that the hell down."

"Yeah, but telling a story isn't the same as actually writing it and having it sound good..."

"You're still making excuses, huh? Doesn't sound like you listened to the moral of your own story."

This leaves me a little speechless. Cassie's remark is far bolder than anything she's ever tossed my way before, bordering on stepping over the boss/employee line into the realm of 'friend' for the first time. She must've seen it in my face, because she quickly waves and adds, "Don't take that the wrong way. I mean, it's none of my business what you do. But I love reading, boss, and I love stories...and that's one hell of a story. You should write it down. Get it published and all. Seriously. Besides," she nods at the letter on the desk. "Your Dad was a published writer and everything, and he thought there was potential there. Was he the kind of guy to pat your back if you didn't deserve it?"

She has a point; I've got to admit. "No, I don't suppose he was. Probably why I never showed him my writing. Think I was afraid he'd be a little too honest with me about how good or bad it was."

Her excellent instincts kick in as she directs me toward a different topic. "Why do you think he never mailed that to you?"

I pick up the letter, staring at those words that speak from across a gulf years. "Well, he had a spotty memory even when he was healthy. A lot like mine, actually. Could've very easily got busy and stuck it in that drawer and forgot about it. Or, maybe his Alzheimer's had been brewing for longer than we thought." I shrug. "Either way...I still got it."

And of course, that makes me wonder, idly, about this store and its odd vibe. In a flight of fancy, I imagine Dad losing this package, leaving it on the bus or at a restaurant, throwing it away by mistake or sending it to the wrong address...but the store drawing the package back to this desk drawer, despite it all.

"So what do you think? Was Michelle a ghost, or a distant cousin, or what?"

My answer comes without hesitation. "I don't think it matters, really. And even if I could find out, I don't think I want to know." I think, then, of strange stories written in journals, stored in a box waiting for me at home, in my office. Stories of this town, stories the likes of which maybe I could write, myself. "Some things are just better left unknown."

"So what about you? You finally ready to write that story the way it needs to be written, so people can read it? Cause I think you need to go home right now and hop to it for a few hours, while I hold down the fort here."

I smile at Cassie, suddenly thinking I'd be very proud, indeed, if my daughter Madi turns out to be like her someday. "Out of curiosity...you don't have any distant cousins named Michelle Titchner, do you?"

Cassie snorts and is about to offer a sarcastic reply when the bell over the front door rings, unceremoniously ending our lunch break. Cassie wipes her hands on her pants, stands and heads to the front counter. "Well, I'm back on the clock. Get out of here before I change my mind."

With that, she offers me a grin hauntingly like the one given to me twenty-three years ago, before ducking through the door to the front. As she approaches the customers at the counter, I look down at my old blue notebook and the letter Dad wrote but never got to send.

"You know," I whisper as I gather them up and stand, "I think I'll do just that."

ABOUT THE AUTHOR

Kevin Lucia is the ebook and trade paperback editor at Cemetery Dance Publications. His short fiction has been published in many venues, most notably with Neil Gaiman, Clive Barker, David Morell, Peter Straub, Bentley Little, and Robert McCammon.

His first short story collection, *Things Slip Through,* was published by Crystal Lake Publishing in November, 2013. He's followed that with the collections *Through a Mirror, Darkly, Devourer of Souls, Things You Need, October Nights,* and the novellas *Mystery Road* and *A Night at Old Webb.* His next book, *The Night Road,* is forthcoming from Cemetery Dance Publications in April 2022.

Other Clifton Heights Titles:

Things Slip Through
Devourer of Souls
Through a Mirror, Darkly
Things You Need
Strange Days
October Nights

Made in the USA
Middletown, DE
11 June 2022

66736938R00106